W9-BTB-725

A Hallie Marsh Mystery

5

San Francisco, Paris, New York, Washington, Santa Fe

Merla Zellerbach

THE A-LIST MURDERS

firefall[tm]

MAIN LIBRARY
Champaign Public Library
200 West Green Street
Champaign, Illinois 61820-5193

First Edition: January 2014

© 2013 Merla Zellerbach, all rights reserved.

No part of this book may be used or reproduced
in any manner whatsoever without specific written
permission, except in the case of brief quotations
embodied in critical articles and reviews.

cover design: BJR/EB

FIREFALL EDITIONS
Canyon California 94516-0189
literary@att.net
www.firefallmedia.com

Library of Congress Cataloging-in-Publication Data
Zellerbach, Merla.
The A-List Murders / by Merla Zellerbach. -- First edition.
pages cm. -- (A Hallie Marsh Mystery ; 5)
ISBN 978-1-939434-04-3
1. Women detectives--Fiction. 2. Self-realization in women--Fiction.
3. Mystery fiction. I. Title.
PS3576.E446A77 2014
813'.54--dc23
                        2013046126

Novels by Merla Zellerbach

The A-List Murders

Dying To Dance

Love To Die For

The Missing Mother

Mystery of the Mermaid

Secrets in Time

Firefall Editions

Rittenhouse Square

Random House

Sugar

Cavett Manor

Love The Giver

The Wildes Of Nob Hill

Ballantine

Love In A Dark House

Doubleday

Wish I had the space to name all who've been so understanding and encouraging over the years. Special thanks to my publisher, Elihu Blotnick for his creative ideas and continuing faith in me, and to my dear, even-tempered husband, Lee Munson, not only for understanding my slavish devotion to my computer, but also for being a wise and sensitive editor.

George Christy is a longtime pal and supporter, and Marlowe Rafelle has my gratitude for marvelous proofing and suggestions. My thanks to beautiful cover girl Susan Tamagni, Athena & Timothy Blackburn for introducing Lee and me to The French Laundry, and to the gracious members of the SFPD.

Debra Dooley, Deborah Strobin and Kathleen Alioto were helpful at supplying party memories, Sharon Litsky & John Sampson have shared their wonderful hospitality, and my buddies at the *Nob Hill Gazette* have always been caring and supportive: Lois, Shara, Claudia, Scott.

A grateful nod to my loving family, my female soul mates, my friends at St. Anthony's, at Glide, at the Coalition on Homelessness, at Compassion & Choices, and to all who care about those less fortunate in the world.

Needless to say, my characters are composites; no one in this book, except an occasional celebrity with his or her real name, is based on a living person.

MZ

THE A-LIST MURDERS

PART 1

— Chapter 1 —
Late September, 2012

TULIP ROSENKRANTZ sat stiffly at her desk, scanning her final proofs. The small philanthropic and society-oriented publication she owned had been hit hard by the recession, but unlike so many local magazines, the *Golden Gate Star* was a survivor.

Delivered free every month to San Francisco's middle and upper income neighborhoods, their 96,000 circulation – reaching almost 290,000 Bay Area readers – remained unchanged.

True, ads were scarcer, stories were shorter, pages were fewer, but none of that mattered to the dedicated readers who flipped through the magazine every month, perusing the photos, hoping to find themselves. To some, getting your picture in the *Star* meant you had "arrived."

The social scene was not unfamiliar to Tulip even before she bought the magazine in 1990, twenty-two years prior. Born in Chicago, her devoutly Christian parents liked to trace their ancestry back to their Dutch, German, Scandinavian, and possibly Jewish ancestor, Erik Rosenkrantz, a 16th century governor of Bergen, Norway.

Tulip's father was a wealthy merchant/importer who sent his five children to parochial schools. His wife, proud of their position in Chicago society, was explicit in teaching her offspring to limit their socializing to "people like ourselves."

Unlike her religious siblings, Tulip considered herself

an agnostic, often mumbling under her breath, "Who cares who created us? Why worry about something we'll never know?"

A dedicated rebel, Tulip Rosenkrantz had broken away from her family to pursue her own beliefs and ideals. Against her parents' wishes, she had divorced her wealthy older husband years ago, and had never remarried.

In lonely moments, she sometimes regretted it.

— Chapter 2 —

TULIP ROSENKRANTZ set down her proofs and stared into her magnifying mirror, almost wishing her plastic surgeon could put back some of what he took off.

Not a wrinkle in sight three weeks after the operation, yet she knew her face appeared drawn and tight. She'd had a choice of doing nothing and looking puffy, or getting cut up and looking pulled – and she'd chosen the latter.

After all, beauty wasn't everything – or so she told herself, still thinking it was. Her plain features were well camouflaged by the large, round, tortoise shell glasses she always wore. Friends often wondered what she looked like without them.

Facial changes, however, were only one of the hard facts of aging. The rest of the world considered a woman of sixty-two "old," yet she was the same person inside. You could dye your hair raven black, as she did, you could use the costliest anti-aging creams, you could even have hand surgery to minimize the veins, but the truth was inescapable. You simply had to adjust to the fact that others considered you en route to the grave – or in her case, the urn.

A knock at the door made her stiffen and stuff her mirror into a drawer. "Enter!" she yelled.

"We have a problem." Fifty-year-old Ellen Goldman, longtime editor of the *Golden Gate Star*, stared at her publisher in dismay.

"It's Andi Douvier. Her personal assistant just called to change this afternoon's photo shoot to 10 a.m. tomorrow. It'll throw everyone off. We've got hair and makeup people coming, Neiman's is sending over an armed guard with earrings for her to model – what do we do?"

"Stay cool, Ellen." Tulip's voice was reassuring; she couldn't afford to panic. "I'll call Neiman's. They know that Andi can be difficult. If she weren't so bleeping rich, people would see more than dollar signs when they looked at her. I sense there's a frightened little girl under all those Chanels."

"Maybe – maybe not." Ellen groaned as she imitated Andi's high-pitched voice. "I'd *adore* to help you and Tulip, sweetie, but you must promise me that the makeup man will apply *individual* eyelashes. I don't care about length – just thickness. And you must send the proofs to my own photographer for touch-up."

And they'll come back with all lines and facial expression removed, thought Tulip. "We still need Andi for tomorrow's shoot – if she doesn't cancel again. It's only 11; maybe I can find someone for today. Close my door and come back in twenty minutes."

"Should I call –?"

"Don't do anything. Just go!"

— Chapter 3 —

AFTER ENTERING the numbers on her iPhone, Tulip heard a ring and a male voice announce, "Redington residence."

"This is Tulip Rosenkrantz from the *Golden Gate Star*. Is Mrs. Redington about?"

"I'm afraid not, Ma'am. You might call the Physical Therapy department at the Veterans' Hospital where she volunteers. Would you like the number?"

"No, thanks, I'll try her cell." She dialed again.

This time a woman answered. "Sara? It's Tulip at the *Golden Gate Star*. Got a minute?"

"Hello, Tulip," said a friendly voice. "Nice to hear from you."

"Thanks, dear, I'll make it brief. We have an emergency. We desperately need a gorgeous woman for a picture shoot this afternoon. Could I entice you to pose for us?"

"Oh, I'm sorry. I'd love to help, but I've a commitment here at the hospital, and patients depend on me. I appreciate the thought, though."

"I understand. It's so last minute. You don't have a photogenic friend who might be free this afternoon, do you?"

"No, I – wait a minute. What about Hallie with the big blue eyes?"

"Hallie Marsh? She's lovely, and she comes from a fine family, but to be honest, I don't want a PR person."

"Hallie sold her Public Relations business," Sara explained. "These days, she's just being a Mommy to her six-month-old son."

"Oh? That's important, because our 'Jewels of the

City' story will feature five women who are not only beautiful, but who give their time and efforts to the community."

Sara laughed. "That's Hallie! She was barely out of labor when she went back to working at St. Anthony's, serving meals to the homeless and whatever else she does there. She's a dedicated volunteer."

"Could you give me her cell?"

"She's home now, Tulip. We chatted earlier. Why don't I call her and have her call you? I promise one of us will get right back to you."

"You're a pussycat, Sara. I'll be waiting."

— Chapter 4 —

DANIEL STUART CASSERLY cooed happily in his playpen while his father, Daniel James "Cas" Casserly, sat beaming. Without a doubt, and his wife Hallie agreed, little Danny was the cutest, sweetest, smartest baby they'd ever seen.

To his parents' surprise, Danny rarely cried. He would sometimes lie in his crib for hours with an unwavering stare that made his mother sure he was pondering $E=mc^2$… at the very least.

At the time, however, Hallie was pondering her friend Sara Redington's surprise call. The *Star* had a longtime policy of not running pictures of publicists, and her likeness had never appeared in the popular monthly. Yet now that she had sold her PR business, was she suddenly "respectable" and deserving of this photographic honor?

Thinking it over, she knew that Edith Marsh, her beloved but bossy mother, would not approve. The old adage about keeping your name out of the papers except for birth, marriage and death, was a rule her mother tried to observe – with little success. To her mind, Hallie's twelve-year PR career of trying to insert her clients' names and faces in the media, was, in a word, "abhorrent."

But Hallie had a way of listening to "Mumsy" – as her brother Rob once christened his anything-but-a-Mumsy mother – then ignoring the maternal advice and doing exactly as she pleased.

Rob Marsh idolized his big sister. He wouldn't care if she appeared naked on the cover of *Time* – well, maybe in a bathing suit, since she'd lost her boobs to breast cancer some years ago – though no one who saw her dressed would ever know.

Personally, Rob welcomed publicity. His jazz trio was always looking for gigs, so he was pleased to get a band mention anywhere.

Also, Hallie's journalist husband, Dan "Cas" Casserly, had recently become the owner/publisher of *City Talk* magazine, and might enjoy seeing his wife's picture in the *Star*. His weekly publication had a news format, and Tulip's "society rag," as he called it, was not a competitor.

Even more important to Hallie was the fact that Tulip Rosenkrantz was a woman she liked and respected, both as a friend and as a leader in the community. It occurred to her that Tulip might even feel grateful enough to do a story on St. Anthony's.

"You support my cause and I'll support yours," were the unspoken rules for San Francisco's social philanthropy game – and no one played it better than Tulip.

Besides, baby Danny had a pretty blonde nanny he liked, Cas was traveling, and she had no plans for the rest of the day…so why not indulge herself?

PART 2

— Chapter 5 —

NOT FAR FROM HALLIE'S HOUSE, Alexandra "Andi" Douvier sat at her elegant dressing table, frowning. Why on earth had she accepted a lunch date for the day after the Symphony Opening? And thank goodness her personal assistant/social secretary, Francie Fisher, had postponed the photo appointment at the *Star*.

Andi told herself she should be staying home today, resting. As always at these first-night events, photographers and paparazzi had swarmed around her and her handsome husband of five years, Nick Demetropoulos.

The shot of them entering the large white tent next to Davies Symphony Hall had graced the front page of the morning *Chronicle*. In rare moments, Andi was glad she had married Nick; he knew just the right instant to gaze at her adoringly.

Most of the time, however, her not-so-beloved husband was either at his office, playing psychologist to a handful of rich neurotics, or off screwing one of his mistresses. And thank God for them! Sex was so messy, and never failed to ruin her coiffure. Besides, at fifty-two, who needed it?

Peering into the mirror, Andi began dabbing foundation on her chin. She was attractive in a superficial way, with short, silver-streaked chestnut hair, large brown eyes and flawless skin, thanks to Botox and her cosmetic dermatologist.

Her features might even be called pretty if her expression had a smattering of warmth. But Andi's purposely-cool façade served her well, protecting her from hangers-on and would-be friends with their hands out – or so she often sus-pected.

A professor at Barnard had once corrected her state-ment that, "Sometimes I wish I weren't one of the hoi polloi." He explained that while many used the term to mean the wealthy elite, "hoi polloi" actually meant just the opposite, the "working class." After that, Andi enjoyed correcting any-one and everyone who misused the expression.

Still regretting she'd made a lunch date with the wife of a software CEO who'd just bought a $25 million mansion nearby, Andi resumed painting her face.

The realization that she had to do her own lashes frustrated her, and at the same time, her frustration bothered her even more. As she often did, she thought back to the time when she was a high school senior, vacationing with friends at Lake Tahoe.

On the beach, one day, she met a young doctor from Los Angeles. They chatted and flirted for an hour or so, then he said he had to leave to catch a plane and asked when he could see her again. She was evasive, so he reached for her arm, slipped off the gold bracelet she was wearing, and dropped it in his pocket.

"Give it back," she begged.

"You'll have to come to L.A. to get it," he laughed, handing her his card. "Let me know and I'll meet you at the airport." Without another word, he picked up his beach towel and hurried off.

Two weeks later, after pleading with him on the phone to no avail, she took her first airplane ride. Until then, she'd been afraid to fly, but consumed with anger, she managed to control her fears.

Once the plane was in the air, however, a sudden realization struck her. Gazing down at the miles and miles of tiny houses that stretched as far as she could see, her wrath began to dissolve. In such an enormous world, on such a vast planet, with so many people suffering from hunger, diseases, and wars, how petty and self-centered she was to let one silly piece of jewelry eat away at her. The more she thought about it, the more ridiculous it seemed.

Luckily, she hadn't told the doctor to meet her at the L.A. airport. As soon as the plane landed there, she arranged to take the next flight home.

Her bracelet arrived in the mail a month later, but by that time she no longer cared. The shrewd doctor had unwittingly taught her an invaluable lesson: Look at the rest of the world and don't sweat the meaningless stuff.

And so it was with her eyelashes, too. Tokie, her personal maid, always helped when the makeup man wasn't around, but Tokie had Thursdays off, and the *cosmétique*, as he called himself, had left for Europe. Even Andi's best friend, Megin Dixon, was on a cruise somewhere in the Mediterranean with her boring professor husband. Yet once Andi thought back to the gold bracelet, her frustration faded.

Still, she couldn't help feeling deserted. How was she supposed to squeeze into her new size-four pantsuit with its butt-hugging bottom?

At least three salespersons at Saks had said she looked fabulous in it. And $6,000 wasn't a lot of money for an Akris suit, she told herself, especially when a stunning sleeveless blouse came with it.

She was sure her personal trainer would beam with pride when he saw her. He'd worked so hard helping her build up her biceps and triceps; she was eager to show off her arms. And now, since she always worried about personal safety, he was trying to teach her self-defense, and how to fight off an attacker.

Nevertheless, at 102 pounds, Andi realized that she couldn't do much but scratch him with her long nails and kick the bastard in his manhood.

— Chapter 6 —

ANTON DOUVIER, Andi's beloved father, was a legend in San Francisco. Having spent his life building up the multi-million dollar food company his grandfather founded, Anton had seen scary changes on the horizon.

A longtime widower, he'd had time to get to know his relatives, and to realize, sadly, that none of them was capable of taking over. Health problems forced him to sell his flourishing business shortly before he died in 1998, leaving everything to his only child.

Andi had adored her father, and had seen no reason to take her husband's name, when her own was a source of pride. Her first spouse, the father of her daughter, had helped invest her money wisely before she caught him spending five-figure sums on cocaine, and divorced him.

Husband number two was her "true love" till he died from heart disease. And mate number three, forty-eight year old Nick Demetropoulos – he told friends to pronounce it "dee metropolis" – had been an officer in the Marines after earning his psychology degree.

Aside from his practice, he now served his wife as security guard, escort, party host, chauffeur, and when the occasion called for it, window dressing.

In the beginning, Nick had hoped to have a loving relationship with his wife. She was attractive, only four years older than he, and at times, she could be warm, sensitive, even funny. He knew she was still in love with her late husband, and probably always would be, but he felt confident she would learn to love him, too.

He also knew that her wealth came with a steep price; he called it paranoia, and her obsession seemed to take precedence over all else.

Convinced that she was the ideal kidnap victim, Andi Douvier had the unfortunate habit of changing plans and appointments at the last minute, to foil her imaginary abductors. When Nick questioned her about this practice, which inconvenienced so many, including himself, she replied, "Well, I haven't been kidnapped, have I?"

"No," he'd said. "You haven't been eaten by an albino alligator, either."

She ignored his quip, but his teasing had re-ignited her fears. The next day, she hired round-the-clock security guards to watch their house from a car parked across the street.

Trying to reason with her on the subject, Nick had concluded sadly, was hopeless.

— Chapter 7 —

Hallie Marsh, Andi's replacement for the photo shoot, was quite the opposite about dates and meetings. Compulsively prompt or even early for appointments, an obsession that both pleased and frustrated those who knew her, she arrived a minute before two, in response to Tulip's frantic call.

Headquartered in a former bank building on Montgomery Street, the *Golden Gate Star* was three stories up, and showed vestiges of once-tasteful décor. When the magazine first moved there, two decades prior, Tulip's high-end designer had traded her services for a year of free quarter-page ads. And at the time, the classic Charles Eames furniture and woven carpets she'd chosen, looked smart and stylish.

Yet even with tasteful décor, busy media offices are not known for their neatness. Most of the seven staff rooms now featured crowded bookshelves, overgrown file cabinets, and desks cluttered with electronic gear, coffee mugs, and piles of paper. Constant requests from the publisher to "straighten up" were honored for a few days, then ignored.

By the time Hallie arrived for her photo shoot, Tulip's favorite photographer, Scotty Drew, had moved the reception desk and chairs to one side, and set up an off-white backdrop in the entrance lobby.

Down the hall, Ellen Goldman's editorial quarters had been transformed into a temporary beauty shop. Mirrors, makeup, and hair products covered her desk.

Strangers bustled about, shouting to each other in nervous voices. No one seemed to notice when Hallie appeared, and made her way through the confusion to Tulip's office.

How strange, she thought, to be coming to the *Star* to do the publisher a favor, after years of going there to request favors. At least their meetings always started out that way. Almost inevitably, the arrangement would end up mutually profitable, with Hallie's client buying an ad in the *Star*, providing tickets to a high-priced event, or offering some sort of free service. Without ever referring to their agreement as a "trade," the *Star* would run a photo of the client, or feature the person in the next issue.

Equally often, though, Hallie or a friend had sought help publicizing a cause, and had always found Tulip generous. She not only embraced philanthropy as every citizen's obligation, she knew how much her support of the arts and various charities enhanced the paper's reputation.

"We *report* social events," she liked to say, "but we *promote* nonprofits."

— Chapter 8 —

DRESSED IN HER TRADEMARK black turtleneck and slacks, Tulip Rosenkrantz came around her desk to give Hallie an air hug – a brief embrace with arms, not bodies, touching.

Hallie had long admired Tulip's tall figure and stately posture. Broad shoulders and slim hips might make her look somewhat masculine were it not for a seriously ample bosom.

"You're a lifesaver!" Tulip grinned, showing off her 90k porcelain veneers. "I'd ask you into my office for coffee, but the beauty team awaits you." She eyed her guest carefully.

"Of course you're gorgeous just as you are: long, wispy blonde hair, delicate nose, exquisite complexion – and a figure to match. Motherhood agrees with you."

"Why, thanks, Tulip. You've been a good friend over the years. I'm flattered that you called me."

"We'll talk later, pussycat, and you *must* show me pictures of your adorable baby." She pointed. "Scotty's down the hall, first door on the left."

Scotty Drew, a former photojournalist for the Hearst Corporation, had left the newspaper business young enough to start a second career. After opening his own portrait studio, however, he soon realized that taking pictures at social events was far more lucrative – and more fun, too, since he enjoyed meeting people.

In no time, the aspiring photographer began to recognize the faces he snapped, and to know their owners' foibles. This woman would only allow profile shots, that one insisted on combing her hair first, another liked her cleavage showing, and so on. Always gracious, Scotty made it a point to remember his clients' requests – as well as their most flattering angles.

"Turn a bit to the left," he would say, or "Chin up, please," or "Say 'kiss.' " And they loved the results.

Not the least of Scotty's assets was that he posted his work online the night of the event, so that the women – and some men – could admire themselves the next day, and order glossies of the shots for their scrapbooks.

— Chapter 9 —

DESPITE THE FACT that publicists were considered press, and therefore off limits for photographers, Scotty Drew had long admired Hallie's warmth and beauty, and had snapped her on several occasions. Yet as expected, the pictures never found their way into print.

She was delighted to greet him that Thursday afternoon, thinking he looked tired and overworked, and noting, as almost everyone did, his resemblance to a young Elvis Presley.

Well-liked, and much in demand, Scotty had the ability to be charming and personal, and at the same time, passionate about his privacy. Well-meant questions about his wife and children were always answered with three words, "They're fine, thanks."

The shoot took about seventy minutes. Having spent hours watching temperamental talents glamourize her clients, Hallie was prepared to be made up and fussed over *ad nauseam*. She was not disappointed.

The moment the shoot ended, she blew a kiss to Scotty, asked editor Ellen to thank Tulip, then escaped as fast as she could.

Driving home, she felt a sense of relief to be out of the PR business, and never again have to cater to demanding clients and media moguls. Most columnists were glad for "items" from publicists, the majority of TV and radio hosts were relatively pleasant; others were so in love with their own power, they lost touch with who they were.

Fortunately, she thought, the social media had taken over many functions formerly assigned to publicists. Still, egocentric males would always be around, needing flattery and reassurance, as well as insecure females who depended on seeing their names and faces in print in order to feel they mattered.

Thus was it ever…in certain circles.

— Chapter 10 —

ELEVEN DAYS LATER, on the first of October, 2012, and after having changed her appointment twice more, Andi Douvier showed up for the *Star's* monthly photo shoot. Her best friend, Megin Dixon, fresh from the ocean cruise, went with her.

Megin had lost no time falling back into her role of adoring Andi – which she honestly did, considering her the big sister she never had.

Money wasn't a problem. Megin wasn't rich, but she and her law professor husband Elliot lived comfortably in a Pacific Heights condominium. He had convinced her he'd be a terrible father – teaching was his life – and he already had an autistic child from a previous marriage. Reluctantly, Megin had agreed not to have children.

An exceptionally pretty woman of forty-three, with shoulder-length red hair, curious hazel eyes, and a dimpled smile, Megin was proud of her J.D. degree, and had worked her way up to being a partner in a prestigious local firm.

After twenty years, however, the practice of law had

lost its appeal. She'd retired at forty, a decision triggered by Andi's invitation to take a week off and fly with her to Paris. The trip cemented a longtime friendship that had begun years earlier, when Andi walked into Megin's office for her first divorce.

The friendship proved to be mutually advantageous. Andi had an attractive, socially-aware, extremely smart friend she admired and trusted. She didn't need or want many others in her life.

At the same time, Megin found herself and her academic husband in a world they'd never known. The women "at the top" entertained lavishly, often for celebrities and world dignitaries, donated generously to the arts, spent fortunes on their faces and figures, and gave extravagant gifts to their families and friends.

Andi was no exception. She'd bought Megin a black Mercedes for her birthday, and also, she admitted, so that Megin could drive her places. That way, she would no longer have to hire chauffeurs who might whisk her away and sell her to kidnappers.

Both women wore a size four, and when Andi tired of her clothes, which was often, Megin's designer wardrobe grew. Occasionally, Andi would ask Megin to stop at Chanel for a lipstick, or to pick up a $300 jar of Crème de La Mer. In those instances, Andi would always say, "Please get one for yourself, too – from me." And Megin was happy to do so.

Sometimes Megin felt guilty that she'd traded practicing law for a self-indulgent life, and she fully intended to do pro bono work, but at the moment she was too busy. Andi took a great deal of her time, and both she and Megin enjoyed the kind of close, caring female companionship they had never known.

Friends talked about their relationship, sometimes with raised eyebrows, but their intimacy was asexual, and gossip rarely bothered them. Nevertheless, jealousy and pettiness were not unknown at San Francisco's highest levels of society. Megin was well aware that her access to Andi was envied, but she had earned that closeness, and was not about to share it.

Fortunately, Elliot Dixon had a heavy teaching schedule and didn't much care what Megin did during the day, as long as she was home for dinner – even if he was getting tired of Trader Joe's enchiladas.

All considered, Megin's loyalty to Andi was firm and constant, but not unlimited. It was, in one way, quite limited. To be honest with herself, Megin's devotion to her best friend somewhat assuaged her guilt about sleeping with her best friend's husband.

Still, it seemed as if a good part of San Francisco's female population had also slept with Nick Demetropoulos, so what was the harm? Andi had clearly told her – with no regrets – that their sex life was over.

Feeling sorry for the poor neglected husband, Megin's altruistic nature had inspired her to let him know she was available. He'd accepted with alacrity, and showed his gratitude in the way he knew best. So why should she feel guilty?

Besides, he was an awesome lover. After their first tryst, in the apartment he owned for such purposes, she'd gotten dressed and was ready to leave, when he suddenly pulled her back to bed for an encore.

For the next two days…she could barely walk.

— Chapter 11 —

TROUBLE WAS BREWING at the *Golden Gate Star,* the day of Andi's shoot. Shortly after she and Megin left, Ellen discovered that the photo crew had turned her editorial office upside down, spilled coffee on her papers, knocked over her precious orchid plant, and left her desk even messier than before.

No satisfaction ever came from complaining to Tulip, who simply told her to clean it up. And as she always did when Tulip ignored her feelings, Ellen thought about retiring.

Sixteen years of her life was enough. On several such occasions in the past, her boss had always convinced her to stay. But this time Ellen was serious. No matter what perks Tulip dangled in front of her, she would not be talked out of it!

Marching up the hall with determined stride, Ellen knocked on the publisher's door.

"Come in," Tulip called. Her voice was low and gentle, as it always was when she sensed trouble. She pointed to a chair facing her desk.

The editor dutifully sat down. "I think you know why I'm here," she said. "Peter's been nudging me to retire, and I really would like us to have some travel time. It's been a wonderful run and I won't desert you. I'll stay through

29

October – maybe even November, or however long you need me – I certainly want to break in my replacement."

To her astonishment, there was a moment's silence, then Tulip melted into a smile. "I understand, dear. You've done an exceptional job for – how many years?"

"Sixteen."

"You're due to retire, I know, and I'm going to miss you terribly. But I can't be selfish. I appreciate your staying on a bit to help. I'll start looking for someone right away."

"Um – well – that's wonderful. Thanks, Tulip."

Hiding her shock, Ellen rose and hurried out the door.

PART 3

— Chapter 12 —

A MONTH LATER, an expressionless, airbrushed and wrinkle-free Andi Douvier stared out from the cover of the November *Star*. Hallie Marsh's smiling picture was inside the magazine on page three, and it pleased her, especially the mention of her volunteer work at St. Anthony's.

"It's fun to see yourself in the paper," she told Cas that evening. "I phoned Tulip to thank her, and she told me that her editor's resigning. Tulip was thrilled she didn't have to fire her. She wants someone more in touch with the younger crowd."

"Makes sense."

"Tomorrow she's got three people coming, and she asked if I'd sit in on the meetings and give her feedback."

Cas glanced up from his iPad. "Is she paying you?"

"No, I'm acting as a friend."

"You're acting as a consultant. You should be paid."

"I'm glad to help her. I'm curious, too – and flattered that she wants my opinion."

"She's taking advantage."

Hallie smiled. "No, darling, I'm taking advantage of her. I want a big cover spread on my favorite charity."

"Oh." He laughed. "As always, you're ten steps ahead of me."

— Chapter 13 —

THE NEXT AFTERNOON, a Friday, when the *Star's* offices were usually closed, Hallie arrived in time to meet the first applicant for Ellen's job. A young German man with an accent had worked as assistant editor for a financial sheet. His manner was cold, precise, and his goal would be to make the *Star* "more literary like New York and Berlin."

Big mistake.

Number two was a twenty-four-year-old divorcee who'd majored in journalism at City College, and had three children under six. She seemed overwhelmed and exhausted.

The third candidate was a thin woman who wore a "Female Empowerment" T-shirt with tight jeans. Her journalistic experience consisted of having co-authored a set of cookbooks for diabetics.

The moment she left, Tulip sent Hallie a questioning look.

Hallie replied with a thumbs-down. "I wouldn't hire any of them. Hate to be negative, but even I've had more experience than those three put together.

"Oh?" Tulip's face lit up; her plan might be working. "You definitely have. Listen, dear, Ellen's anxious to leave. What would you think of coming in for a few days and serving as interim editor until I hire someone? Right now, it would only be a half-day job, and I'll pay you well."

Hallie laughed. "You couldn't possibly afford me. Are you serious? I'm no editor."

"You could be – and a writer, too. In fact, I desperately need someone to cover Andi Douvier's anniversary party this Saturday. That marriage has lasted five years, to everyone's amazement." She glanced at her datebook. "Oh, dear, it's tomorrow night! I'm going, but I'm no writer. By any chance, are you going?"

33

"I wasn't invited. I don't know Andi. And I'm no writer, either."

"You most certainly are. I've been reading your press releases for years. And anyone's better than Ellen. Her writing's like chewing gum without the flavor. Besides, Andi's hired Scotty Drew for the party, so we'll get plenty of pictures. All you have to do is go there, describe the boat –"

"Boat?"

"It's aboard a yacht. Andi chooses a new venue every year. Take a few notes on who's wearing what, pick up a clever remark or two – that's all we need. It should be a fun cruise around the Bay. Here's the invitation."

Hallie stared at the ornate gold card, and sat speechless. After a long moment, she said, "It sounds quite elegant – except for the dress code: 'Please wear rubber-soled shoes.'"

"Well, the party's one thing. If you can't go, I'll send someone else. What I'm really asking is that you give me a hand in the office for a few days. Come in at eight and you're done by one. Or make your own hours."

"I've no experience –"

"We both know better. You're a whiz at editing copy."

Hallie nodded mechanically, her brain spinning with this sudden challenge. "May I call you tomorrow?"

"Of course, dear. We're closed Saturdays, as you know. Call me at home. It's a fun job, pussycat, and you can tell that handsome husband of yours that it's only till I hire someone permanent."

"Thanks, Tulip. I'm flattered." Hallie grabbed her purse, waved a kiss and left.

— Chapter 14 —

"YOU WANT TO DO *WHAT*?" Cas stared at his wife in amazement. He had just finished a second helping of lasagna.

"I'm tired of staying home."

"Your mother bought us this lovely house so you would stay home and cook for your husband."

"I do cook."

"You cook once a year. And it's always lasagna."

"Picky, picky. Well, now I'd like to play reporter and go to Andi Douvier's party tomorrow night. Then I want to play editor for a few days – maybe a week – just for fun."

Cas paused a moment before speaking. His voice was gentle. "Journalism looks easy, sweetheart, but writing up a party isn't the same as writing a press release. And editing copy isn't the same as being the editor of a 40-page magazine. It may be a half-day job, but it's a huge responsibility."

"I know that," she insisted, "and much as I love our darling Danny, I can't play stay-at-home mother forever. This is a new challenge. PR work is so different. I've been the one chasing after the media for twelve years. Now I'll be on the other side. All my old competitors will be chasing me!"

"Your choice, honey," he said resignedly.

She'd made up her mind. Further efforts to dissuade her, he knew, would be futile.

— Chapter 15 —

THE NIGHT WAS CHILLY – one of those rare San Francisco evenings when the temperature dropped to forty, and the biting cold pierced through Hallie's three layers. Having parked two blocks away, she arrived at her destination on foot, shivering, and clutching her temporary *Star* credentials.

After the many criminals she'd confronted as an amateur detective, and the hundreds of bios and press releases she'd sent out, writing up a society party for all to read made her anxious, and for an instant, sorry she'd said yes. She was certain to see some friends at the party. Would they think she was crazy posing as a reporter?

Just ahead of her, eight empty stretch limos were parked along Washington Street in the city's posh Pacific Heights district. Beside them, a sprawling white Colonial mansion dominated the block. Built by a movie star in the '50s, the showy structure on the city's biggest residential lot was the current home of party host Andi Douvier.

Having seen Megin Dixon's picture in the social pages, Hallie recognized Andi's close friend, standing next to a young person who was probably Francie Fisher, Andi's personal aide. The two women were directing the flow of traffic, as a long line of expensive cars pulled up and deposited their nattily dressed passengers.

Despite the cold, the two greeters smiled cheerfully as they welcomed the guests, checked their names off a list, then steered them to the waiting limos. Blue-jacketed valets whisked away their cars.

Reminding herself of her mission, Hallie approached one of the limo drivers, introducing herself as a reporter. He was happy to inform her that each limo seated twelve, and that the 165-foot yacht "Medusa" awaited ninety-six guests at the Embarcadero Pier. They were to board no later than

7 p.m. for a 7:30 sailing.

"The owner's a friend of Miss Douvier's," the man explained. "I hear he's had four big-bucks divorces, and thinks all women are part-reptile – like the lady with the snakes coming out of her head."

"Yes, I know about Medusa." Hallie thanked him and hurried up to meet Megin and Francie. They welcomed her warmly, as a reporter for the *Star*, and directed her to Limo #9, where she sat with three other magazine writers, and Carolyne Bigelow from the *Chronicle*. Scotty Drew and his assistant, and four security guards, were also passengers in what the lively group promptly christened, "The Freebie Coach."

— Chapter 16 —

ALTHOUGH IT WAS ONLY NOVEMBER, the "Medusa" sat proudly in the San Francisco harbor, glowing like a giant Christmas tree. Boughs of red carnations, intertwined with colored lights and green Satsuma branches, wound around three freshly-painted decks. As the limos pulled up to the dock, guests stepped onto a red carpet that continued up the gangplank.

At the top, Hallie's fellow passengers instantly deserted her. Scotty Drew and his aide separated and began snapping away, the guards scurried to their assigned posts, the reporters began texting. She felt like a rookie, scribbling in her notebook, but for her first and hopefully last attempt at journalism, she didn't want any technical problems.

A portly, bearded Captain in full dress white uniform,

stood just inside the entrance greeting guests. Beside him, in a pink cashmere jumpsuit with matching rubber boots – smiling Andi Douvier doled out double-cheek air kisses.

A few steps past them, lean, dark-haired Wallace Robinson, everyone's favorite butler and sometimes bartender, stood tall in his tuxedo. His elegant appearance, from his perennially suntanned face down to his black Ferragamo loafers – rubber-soled as instructed – made him easily identifiable. He bowed slightly as he welcomed guests by their last names, and handed their wraps to a waiting attendant.

If Wallace Robinson didn't recognize you and know your drink, you were nobody who mattered – at least, not in San Francisco. He'd often seen Hallie at her mother's parties, and once told her, "I know enough secrets to blackmail everyone in this room." He'd laughed when he said it, then added, "But I'd rather stay alive."

Ignoring her stomach flutters, Hallie smiled bravely and stepped up to the host, who hugged and welcomed her as if she were one of the guests. Apparently assuming she was, Andi had no interest in hearing her name, and went on to the next arrival. The Captain looked Hallie in the eyes, as he was trained to do, mumbled a welcome and shook her hand. So much for the receiving line.

"Ms. Marsh, what a lovely surprise!" Wallace brightened as Hallie hurried toward him. It was futile, she knew, to ask him to call her by her first name. She had tried too many times.

"I'm not a real guest," she whispered. "I'm a lowly reporter doing a favor for Tulip."

"Lucky Tulip," he whispered back, then went into his

usual spiel. "Welcome aboard, Count and Countess Émile de Baubery. Don't you look divine!"

The Count walked on, ignoring Wallace to grab a glass of champagne from a server. The Countess mumbled, "Thanks, Wallace," and paying no attention to her wandering spouse, headed for a circle of friends.

Hallie moved away to jot notes. Everyone knew that Babe de Baubery, a strikingly beautiful brunette, had modeled lingerie for Victoria's Secret until the Count spotted her semi-nude picture in the catalogue.

Rumor had it that she dated him for months, withholding sexual favors until the poor man proposed. She promptly wed her much older admirer, instantly metamorphosed from Beatrice Brown to Countess Babe de Baubery, and almost overnight, rose to the top of the uber-exclusive social-celebrity list.

Currently, she served on the War Memorial Board of Trustees, chaired the Opening Night's Opera Ball, and managed to have her name and picture appear regularly in almost every local, national, and international society column.

Hallie remembered Babe was once quoted in the *Star* saying something like, "San Francisco is such a small town. You don't have to be born with money to be 'in', but you need to have it. An aspiring 'nouvelle' might pay five figures for an Opera gown, but old money knows that the secret is to be on the Grand Benefactor list."

And Babe was shrewd enough – and rich enough – to do both.

— Chapter 17 —

WHEN THE LAST of the guests arrived at 7:35, the hatch was closed, engines purred, and the ship was underway. The receiving line dissolved, late arrivals melted into mingling.

Wallace, the butler, noticed Hallie scribbling in a corner. "Put away that notebook," he scolded, as he passed by. "Get out there and act like you're a guest. That's the only way you'll get a story."

"You're right," she said resignedly.

His advice was appreciated, but she'd still make notes. Since the guests had all disappeared down the passageway, she grabbed her pen and wrote:

"*The Countess walks and stands like the fashion model she used to be. Babe de Baubery wins first prize for posture, but a frown from a ship's officer, who has just noticed her five-inch stilettos. He whispers in her ear, she smiles sweetly, reaches into her Hermès Birkin Bag for a pair of espadrilles, then holds them up for all to see. Scotty Drew grabs his camera and dashes over to record the thrilling event.*"

Whoops! Skip the sarcasm, Hallie told herself, dropping the notepad into her purse. Taking a deep breath, she glanced around for the first time, noting her surroundings.

"You lost, Miss?"

"Oh, uh, I'm a reporter, sir – officer. I'm just trying to describe the ship."

The short blond man with a Greek accent clicked his heels and saluted. "At your service, Madame. I am Chief Engineer Giorgio. May I show you our Brazilian teak deck?"

"Why, yes…thank you."

Taking her arm, he led her down the passageway, through glass doors to the outside. "As you know," he said, speaking as if reading a brochure, "the Medusa – named to dishonor the owner's fifth wife – was designed and built for Mr. Nestor Panagiotis, a Greek businessman."

"She was launched in 1973," he rattled on, "and completely refurbished in 2007. She's 165 feet long, has a crew of twenty-four, three large teak decks, a 45-foot beam and nine-foot ceilings. Her twin screws are powered by twin diesel engines. The furnishings feature rare woods, expert stonemasonry and carved moldings, hand-woven carpets, and modern art worth more than the yacht."

"Wow."

"As you will see," he continued, leading her back inside, "we are very proud of the ornamental details on the mahogany paneling. The ceiling beams –"

"Beautiful," she interrupted, noting the crystal chandeliers and wondering how they'd weather a rough sea. The heavily varnished paintings on the walls looked garish and tasteless. "I really came to write about the party. Would that be down this hall?"

"Yes, starboard at the end of the passageway. You should also know that we have climate control and iPad multimedia systems hidden behind the paneling and the mirrors. I can take you below and show you."

"Thanks, but –"

"You see, Mr. Panagiotis knew Aristotle Onassis in the early seventies, and even though Onassis was older and richer, Mr. P. was determined to build a bigger and more elaborate yacht than the *Christina*. He copied several Onassis touches, such as a mosaic floor on the swimming pool, and covering his bar stools with fine leather made from the minke whale's foreskin."

That did it. Time to escape her chatty guide whose increasing hold on her arm hinted he might have other ideas about where she should spend the evening. Pulling away, Hallie called over her shoulder, "Thanks, officer. I have work to do."

— Chapter 18 —

HALLIE HAD NO TROUBLE following the noise and music to the "Gorgon Ballroom." What a horrible name, she thought, remembering from her Smith College days that Medusa was a "gorgon" – a monstrous snake-haired woman who turned everyone who looked at her into stone. Hallie had no desire to meet the ship's vengeful owner, Mr. Panagiotis – nor any of his five discarded wives.

The ballroom looked stuffy and crowded. A moment after entering, she turned her back and wrote, "Mr. P. never heard of Mies van der Rohe's 'Less is more' philosophy."

Indeed, the edges of the room were lined with Lucite urns filled with large red roses. Painted murals covered the walls. Giant crystal chandeliers dangled from the ceiling, spotlighting the gold-linen-covered tables. Servers, dressed as Greek gods and goddesses, passed trays bulging with drinks and hors d'oeuvres, while a 10-piece band played Greek songs and dance music.

After wandering about and making notes on various guests, Hallie was approached by a male deity – or reasonable facsimile. "Caviar *en panier?*" he asked, offering a tray of tiny pastry baskets.

"Hate the stuff," she wanted to say, then smiled. "No thanks. Would you happen to know where this ship is going?"

"Yes, Madame. This is a three-hour cruise on the Bay. We start by sailing past Alcatraz Island, over to Treasure Island and the Bay Bridge. Then we come west to circle Angel Island, pass Tiburon and Sausalito, where you'll see the sparkling San Francisco lights against the illuminated skyline. We go out under the Golden Gate Bridge for a spell on the Pacific Ocean, and come back beneath the bridge. Then we sail along the Embarcadero to the pier where we dock."

"Wonderful!" He had memorized his speech well. "Thanks."

"Happy to be of help." He checked his watch. "It's 8:30 already. We serve dinner at 9."

"Sit-down?"

"Yes, on the upper deck. Please get your table number from one of the hostesses."

Strolling through the crowd again, Hallie chatted with a few acquaintances, mostly her mother's friends, who were friendly until they spotted someone higher up on the social scale.

Tulip Rosenkrantz greeted her warmly, introduced her as "Edith Marsh's daughter," then whispered in her ear, "Go mingle."

Mingle, shmingle. Hallie cursed mentally as she continued her path across the ballroom. Most of her thirty-six years she'd spent working, building up her successful PR business, donating much of her time to nonprofits, avoiding the party scene. A strong devotee of the arts, she supported them because she enjoyed them, not to be a boldface name in the social pages.

It was unfortunate, she reflected, that her PR colleagues – always at the mercy of the media – often had low self-esteem. Recently, a former associate, trying out for a TV quiz show, caught her eye. Asked her profession, the publicist replied, "I'm a multi-media management consultant."

No one knew what she meant and she was promptly bumped as a contestant. Served her right, Hallie thought. How could people respect the creativity and hard work the PR profession demanded, if the people in it were ashamed to say what they did?

— Chapter 19 —

A CHEERY VOICE broke into Hallie's reverie. "I don't believe it! You accepted Tulip's offer?"

"I was curious. I wanted to see one of Andi's fabled parties. And we're prisoners here for three hours!" Hallie hugged her friend Sara Redington. "You don't know how glad I am to see you. What a snooty crowd!"

"Shhh! Of course they're snooty. That's what this is all about. No amount of money could buy an invitation to one of Andi's parties. And an amazing thing happens at these events. People who wouldn't normally give you a second look, suddenly greet you with smiles and air kisses. 'If you're at Andi's party, hey, you must be okay – i.e. one of us.' "

44

"Ah, yes. The A-crowd. Tell me something I can write about. By the way, where's your handsome husband?"

"Dale didn't want to, quote, waste an evening, un-quote. I came with friends. They told me about their neighbor who was so mortified that she wasn't invited, she hid her car in her son's garage so people would think she was out of town."

"You made that up."

"No, it's true! Come on, I'll introduce you to Dagmar Millard. She chaired the Symphony Gala last month – a real dynamo, and she's great copy."

PART 4

— Chapter 20 —

THE SHIP'S CLOCK struck nine bells – time to dine. Pretty hostesses in navy-and-white sailor dresses bustled through the crowd, making sure all the guests had their table numbers, then ushering them up to the next deck for dinner.

Having reluctantly left Sara, Hallie hurried up the ladder, checked her assigned seat, and was pleased to find herself back with the photographers and reporters. "Welcome to the freebie section," she mumbled, half to herself.

Ten round tables, each elegantly set for ten guests, filled a smaller, more compact ballroom. The decor was sparse, a welcome contrast to the lower deck. In the center of each table, two small white lovebirds flapped about in faux tortoise shell cages.

"You don't think they'd seat us with their invited guests, do you?" asked photographer Scotty Drew.

"I guess it beats eating in the kitchen." Hallie fanned her face with her napkin. "They've sure got that heat turned up."

"Ships don't have kitchens," he corrected, snapping a picture of a pretty server in a white toga. "They have galleys."

"Authors have galleys, too," growled Joel Jones, a pony-tailed writer for *Wealth* magazine. He turned his eyes to the truffle and crab legs salad on his plate. "I'm starved. Can we eat?"

"I'm told we have to wait till the host says a few words." Hallie reached for her glass. "But we can drink. Here's to us!"

Joel emptied his goblet and wiped his forehead. "I'm as sweaty as a Sumo wrestler's armpit. It's a bloody oven in here!"

— Chapter 21 —

AFTER WAITING TWENTY MINUTES for Andi Douvier to welcome her guests, the hungry crowd picked up their forks. A moment later, across the room at a long head table, a hunched-over man with squinty eyes rose to his feet. He tapped his glass for silence and finally got it.

"Dear Friends," he began, in a raspy voice, "on behalf of the lovely Alexandra Douvier, I welcome you to planet Medusa. My name is Nestor Panagiotis, and I have the honor and pleasure of owning this charming vessel. My staff is here to answer your every wish and desire. Dear Andi will be with us shortly, but for now, please relax, enjoy the special wines from my private cellar, and Chef Gaston's superb cuisine. *Gia sou...bon appétit!*"

Hands clapped, glasses clinked. One table began to chant, "We want Andi! We want Andi!" and was promptly shushed by an officer.

"Where the hell is she?" asked Joel, digging into his salad. "Probably OD'ed on coke."

Hallie looked startled. "She uses cocaine?"

"So I hear."

"How awful! Isn't that horribly expensive?"

"You gotta be kidding. That would be piggy bank change to Andi Douvier. Anyway, stuff is cheaper than it was," said Joel. "You can buy an eight-ball of coke – three and a half grams of powder – for about two hundred bucks. And that's for the sparkly good stuff, not the dull stuff that wrecks your nose."

Hallie frowned. "Sounds terrible."

"Smart girl. The high is fantastic but it only lasts thirty to forty minutes, and the crash is pure hell. That's why people try it out of curiosity and end up getting addicted."

"Have you –?"

"I'm a sporadic user. Those of us who can use occasionally without getting hooked, have bigger brains. Honestly! It's scientific. Addicts have smaller frontal lobes. We...hey! What the –?"

He was staring at the table centerpiece. A white dove was lying on her side, motionless. The other was on her back, feet in the air. Joel reached into the cage and quickly withdrew his hand.

"Holy shit!" he yelled. "I knew it was hot in here. Those birds are *dead*!"

Word spread quickly. Commotion ensued. With all the food, wine, and chatter, it seemed as if none of the guests had noticed that the doves had all perished, most likely from the heat.

Within minutes, officers, sailors, and hostesses appeared on the scene. Grabbing the cages as fast as they could, they loaded them onto metal carts and wheeled them out of sight.

Chapter 22

"LADIES AND GENTLEMEN, may I have your attention!" The Captain's strong voice, fifteen minutes later, was a command, not a request.

Dining room chatter stopped instantly.

"I am sorry to report that we have a minor engine problem, and much to our regret, we are changing our course and returning to port. Miss Douvier, Mr. Panagiotis and I urge you to enjoy the rest of your meal, and perhaps a glass or two of ouzo. Starting now, the lower deck is open for dancing. We should be in San Francisco in about twenty-five minutes. Thank you for your cooperation."

Sudden silence greeted the end of his announcement, then just as suddenly came a clamor of voices.

"What the hell's going on?" asked Joel. "The Captain's not telling us a friggin' thing. Something's very wrong, and where in God's name is Andi? I hope to hell we make it back."

Hallie began jotting notes. Scotty stared at her. "What are you writing?" he asked. "Nothing's happened yet."

Joel laughed and turned to the cameraman. "You remind me of the cub reporter who was sent to cover this high society wedding. He went there and came right back to his editor. 'The groom was a no-show,' he said, 'so there was no story.' "

"My point exactly." Hallie set down her pen to glance around the room. "The passengers are nervous, the ship's turning back, no one knows what's going on, and the host has disappeared into cyberspace. This could be big news!"

— Chapter 23 —

EXPLAINING THAT SHE WAS OFF to find out more about the dead birds, Hallie excused herself from the table and set out for the bridge. As she was about to exit the ballroom, a man's voice called out, "Leaving so soon?"

She spun around to see a tall, attractive stranger. Dark brown hair framed an unusually handsome face. White slacks under a navy blazer hugged a slim, muscular body.

"I'm Nick," the man said, approaching with an outstretched hand. "I'm sort of the host tonight and I'm trying to find my table."

"Sort of?"

"Well, it's really my wife Andi's party – the A-list, you know? My pals are mostly D-list. You must be one of her friends, but you don't look like the stuck-up type. You're quite lovely. Where's she been hiding you?"

Hallie smiled sweetly – as if she didn't know Nick Demetropoulos's reputation. "I met your wife for the first time tonight. I'm doing a story for the *Golden Gate Star*."

"Wonderful! I'll show you around the ship."

That seemed to be the pickup line of the evening. "Thanks, but I was hoping to find out what's happening. Any idea where your wife is?"

"Last I heard, she was off crying about the lovebirds. It's our anniversary and she's quite sentimental." He gave a shrug. "She has a thing for doves. When she was little, her father told her Douvier was the French word for a man who raised doves. It's baloney, but she believes it."

51

"I'm so sorry they died. I didn't think the heat was that bad. Would she still be with the birds?"

He stared in surprise. "Didn't she come back? Isn't she sitting at the Captain's table with that ass Panagiotis?"

"No. She's missing."

"From what?"

"From the party, apparently."

"Oh, hell, she's probably passed out in a rowboat." He grabbed a card from his pocket and thrust it in Hallie's hand. "Call me," he said, and hurried back to the tables.

— Chapter 24 —

ASKING VARIOUS PERSONS along the corridor, Hallie found her way up to the bridge, on the ship's highest deck. Ignoring the "No Admittance" sign, she opened the door quietly and shut it behind her. Across the floor, the Captain and another officer stood with their backs to her, staring out the bow through four panes of wraparound window.

A few feet behind them, a helmsman held the wheel. Charts were strewn across a narrow table. Tension filled the air.

Outside, the sky was black and starless, lit only by two giant searchlights on either side of the bow, scanning the water.

"We've checked every inch of the ship – twice," she heard the officer tell the Captain. "The Coast Guard has a full description, the time Miss Andi was last seen, plus latitude and longitude. They'll be searching the water around Angel Island. Her friend Margaret said –"

"Megin."

"Yessir. Megin said Miss Andi had been drinking and possibly taken some medication."

"You mean drugs?"

"Possibly. I couldn't find her husband, he –"

Hallie took a long breath and cleared her throat. "Hate to burst in, Captain," she said, pretending to be breathless. "I came to tell you the passengers are quite frightened. Tempers are barely under control and your presence and your reassurance are badly needed."

"Thanks, Miss," he snapped. "I'll tend to it. Now please go. You shouldn't be in here."

"Sorry." She left hastily, stopping around a corner to add to her notes. The situation was worse, but the story kept getting better. Andi Douvier overboard? Accident? Suicide? Everyone knew she had a fixation about being kidnapped. She'd been seen dancing and drinking when they first sailed, but if she'd been on drugs as well, and at some point walked the wet, slippery deck, she might easily have lost her footing.

And yet, a heavy railing separated the ship from the treacherous night waters. For Andi to fall into the water, someone would have had to lift her and push her over that steel barrier. Murder? Who would do such a thing? Who would go out there in the cold? And who would want Andi dead?

As Hallie quickened her step, heading down to the ballroom, a voice boomed over the fog horns: "Your attention, please! This is your Captain speaking. Although we are heading back to port, I hasten to reassure you that the ship is one hundred percent seaworthy, and there is absolutely no danger to anyone aboard. Unfortunately, your host, Miss Douvier, had a minor fall and is resting comfortably in her cabin. She asks that you all continue to enjoy yourselves. Thank you for your cooperation."

— Chapter 25 —

ONE BY ONE, grasping the wooden handrail, the noisy, well-lubricated passengers hurried down the gangplank to the pier. Laughing and talking in loud voices, they seemed happy, and relieved to be on solid ground. A hundred yards away, a bevy of limo drivers beckoned them. No special seats for special people this time. As soon as one car filled, another pulled up.

Hallie was among the last to step off the gangplank, followed by the amiable guest-greeter Wallace, who caught up with her.

"Did you see Andi disembark?" she asked, in a low voice.

He shook his head. "No, Ms. Marsh. If she was ill, they would've had an ambulance waiting. Resting in her cabin? I don't think so. I'll bet she got drunk and went for a swim. If she's really missing, they should've called the police."

"Why didn't they?"

"I'm guessing that if the police came to meet the ship, they'd have kept all the guests, officers, crew, caterers – every-one – holed up on board while they questioned them, maybe even for a day or two. I'll bet anything Ms. Dixon told the Captain not to call the police."

"I saw Ms. Dixon – Megin – and her husband get off. Megin looked worried. Andi's husband Nick was with them. He looked like he was trying to look worried."

Wallace laughed. "Mr. D's not a bad guy. Always takes the time to stop and chat with me. Who cares if he's sleeping with half the female population? His wife couldn't care less. Strangely, in his own way, I think he loves her. He's very protective of her."

"In his own way," she murmured.

"Ms. Douvier's okay, too," Wallace went on. "You have to understand her. She's a lost soul. Deep down she knows it's all about money, so she thrives on being a social icon, and loves to see her name in print. Makes her feel she's somebody."

"Thanks, Dr. Freud."

"I've studied her, Ms. Marsh. She gives away thousands of dollars to good causes, but she's never done a stitch of work except sitting on some art boards. Her maid, Tokie, talks to me. Andi treats her well, but Tokie says she never lets up on her paranoia about being kidnapped. Tokie even had to secretly buy her a gun. Can you imagine sleeping with a loaded gun under your pillow?"

"No! That's insanity!"

He took her arm as they walked. "Did you get a chance to look around the yacht?"

"Yes. I was underwhelmed."

"I'd have liked to get out on deck, but I had to help the caterers clean up. Once we started on the dishes, I never got out of the galley."

"You didn't miss much." Dropping her pen in her purse, Hallie thanked Wallace for having encouraged her to circulate, and excused herself to hurry to the nearest limo.

The other reporters would be busily sending in their copy for the early editions, but the end of the story was yet to be told. Where *is* Andi Douvier? Was she hiding somewhere on the ship? Did she really take a spill? Did she drown? Was she pushed?

The answer, Hallie suspected, would soon be forthcoming.

PART 5

Chapter 26

"WELCOME HOME, SWEETHEART. How was the boat ride?"

Cas greeted his wife with a hug, at the same time, checking his watch. "You're back early. Was it fun?"

"No, it was hard work. I've decided one journalist in the family is enough. How's Danny?"

"Sleeping like an angel."

Hallie kissed her husband's cheek. "He *is* an angel, like his Daddy. I'm going to transfer my notes to my iPad, and they'll explain why I'm home early. Will you proof them before I shoot them off to Tulip?"

"Go for it!"

An hour or so later, Cas entered his wife's office. "Thanks for sending me your copy, honey, it's pretty good for a first attempt. You had a bit of excitement on board."

"Is my story okay?"

"I took the liberty of rewriting parts of it. And since tonight is November third, and *The Star* won't be publishing this until December, you may want to focus on the party and the people – not on Andi's disappearance."

"You're thinking that by December first, we'll know what happened to Andi and it'll be old news?"

"People that well-known don't just disappear. It seems logical that either Andi or her body will turn up in the next week or so."

"Then I have your permission to snoop around?"

"No, but you're going to do it anyway. Right now, though, you've got an exclusive. Send Tulip your copy and she can update it as necessary. I'm sending the story to my editor. It's probably already on the evening news."

"You'd better credit the *Golden Gate Star*."

"Yeah, sure – when elephants fly."

— Chapter 27 —

CAS WAS RIGHT about the story's media appeal. As he and Hallie watched the late news, a bulletin interrupted the broadcast to report the "mysterious disappearance" of heiress Alexandra "Andi" Douvier. Anyone with information was asked to call the police.

The next morning, the *Chronicle's* Sunday headline read: "**Socialite Vanishes!**"

Hallie scanned the story: much speculation, plenty of names and pictures, few details. Holding seven-month-old Danny in her arms, she was more concerned about her son's slight fever, his crying and fussing. Their pediatrician made house calls, but not on weekends. Reached by phone, the doctor suggested giving Danny half a Benadryl, and he soon drifted off to sleep.

No sooner had she put him down, than the phone rang. "It's Helen Kaiser," announced the caller, "am I disturbing you?"

"Not at all." Hallie's voice rose with excitement. The SF Police Department's Lieutenant Helen Kaiser, head of the Homicide Detail and Cas's longtime love interest before he met Hallie, had become a good friend. "I think I know why you're calling."

"Indeed you do, Hallie. I received Andi Douvier's

guest list last night and you're on it. I thought you hated those society bashes."

"I don't hate them, I just try to avoid them. Actually, I was there to write up the party for a friend. Any news about Andi?"

"No. Three of my lab technicians and half a dozen detectives are on the ship now, gathering clues. Can you can come down to the station and tell me your version of what happened?"

"You're working on a Sunday?"

"We're open twenty-four-seven. The media are driving us crazy – plus the Mayor's office."

Hallie looked across the room. Danny was snoozing peacefully in his crib, and Jenny, his Norwegian nanny, sat absorbed in her knitting. Cas was immersed in his iPad. "I'll be there in an hour."

— Chapter 28 —

HALLIE WAS ALWAYS EXCITED to enter the Lieutenant's office at the downtown Hall of Justice. Except for pictures of two young women, probably her nieces, Helen's desk was as uncluttered as her mind. Her thinking was sharp, her speech frank and explicit, with rarely an extra word. Hallie knew her as a stern policewoman with a bright wit but little time for frivolity.

Sparse furniture, save for a desk, some chairs, and wall-to-wall file cabinets, added to the impression that the occupant was tightly wired. How strange, Hallie mused, that her sweet, easygoing, and somewhat lazybones husband had once been this woman's lover.

Helen Kaiser, Hallie knew, was nine years older than Cas at the time of their affair, and probably still was. The two were together in the early days of their careers, when Cas was Bureau Chief for the Associated Press in Washington, and Helen was a newspaper reporter. His drinking, he later admitted, broke them up. Not until he fell in love with Hallie, however, did he begin to honor his AA vows.

Before they married, Cas told Hallie about the relationship, and explained that a few months after they'd ended it, Helen had surprised everyone by leaving the newspaper to attend the Police Academy. Despite warnings, teasing, and ridicule from her fellow journalists, she graduated from the Academy with honors, joined the force, proved herself worthy of constant promotions, and today, the Lieutenant was rumored to be a candidate for Chief.

Having worked with her on several cases, Hallie knew she lived up to her reputation for being tough, detail-oriented, honest and fair. She was also quite a handsome woman, with clear skin and sharp, regular features. Prematurely gray hair was cut short, like a man's, and brushed back off her face.

A gunshot wound when she was walking the beat, had left the Lieutenant with a slight limp, but she worked out at the police gym, determined to stay slim.

She rose when Hallie appeared in her doorway.

"Thanks for coming, have a seat," was her greeting, as she handed Hallie a printed sheet. "Megin Dixon supplied the guest list. Do you know all these people?"

"I know who most of them are, but I can count my

friends on one hand: Sara Redington, Tulip Rosenkrantz, the photographer Scotty Drew, the butler-bartender Wallace Robinson, and the *Chronicle's* Carolyne Bigelow. To my knowledge, none of the guests would have any reason to harm Andi."

"So noted. I'm going to read their names. Tell me whatever you know about them – anything – no matter how trivial."

— Chapter 29 —

THIRTY MINUTES LATER, when the two women had finished, Helen set down the paper. "Why didn't the Captain call us and report Andi missing?" she asked. "We'd have met the ship and questioned everyone aboard. This way makes extra work, and none of the guests can leave town."

"Whew! That's a tough order just before the holidays."

"Too bad. All we know is that the last person to see Andi alive was an officer named Giorgio who met her in the passageway and directed her to her cabin. He said she was wobbly, but didn't want any help."

"She had a cabin?" asked Hallie.

"Yes. According to Megin, Andi and Nick were planning to stay on the ship for two weeks after the party, and have a second honeymoon in – would you believe separate cabins?"

"I – uh, think they have an understanding."

"Oh, yes." Helen rolled her eyes. "I know about Mr. De – whatever-his-name. Husbands are the first suspects, but

Megin told me Andi has an ironclad pre-nup. All he gets from her estate is a living allowance from her trust. The rest goes to her philanthropies and a little to her daughter whom she hasn't seen since she left home in 1995."

"You mean Nick's better off with Andi alive?"

"Apparently. Thanks to her, he's been living the good life. Megin, too. Both seem distraught. We'll check their stories."

Hallie was thoughtful a few seconds before remarking, "Sounds as if you're convinced of foul play, Helen. What about suicide? An accident?"

"The Medical Examiner handles suicides, natural deaths, drug overdoses. My detail investigates any deaths the M.E. deems suspicious. So until we find her body and determine the exact COD, we're treating this as a homicide."

"Everyone keeps talking about Cause Of Death. What if Andi's not dead? Any chance I could get a pass from you to go aboard the ship and look around?"

"Okay, your observations might be helpful. But don't be a nuisance." She reached for a pad on her desk, wrote a few lines and handed her the paper. "I have a meeting now. Would you tell everything you know to Detective Baer?"

Hallie laughed. "I'm sure he'll be thrilled to see me."

— Chapter 30 —

THE SARCASTIC PREDICTION proved more than accurate. Theodore "Teddy Bear" Baer, the overworked detective Hallie had helped solve several murders, was not her fan. He once told her he "tolerated" her because she had some good ideas, but her place was home baking cookies.

Several years earlier, Lieutenant Kaiser had assigned him to a case Hallie was working on, warning her that, "Everyone calls him 'TB.' Don't call him 'Teddy Bear' if you want to live."

And although she knew he preferred "Detective Baer," she'd learned that she could get away with "TB," particularly when she had information he needed.

"So – looks like I'm stuck with you again." TB's sour greeting, plus the fact that he resented having to rise from his comfortable chair to shake her hand, did not dismay her.

At first glance, he seemed even taller than she remembered, towering over six feet. She recognized that same flushed complexion, the nose that looked as if it ran into a wall, the gravelly voice and surprisingly sturdy handshake.

His smile and teasing tone hadn't fooled her the first time they met, and didn't fool her now. His eyes were steely cold. They seemed to penetrate her thoughts.

"Glad to see you, too, TB." She smiled back.

He wasted no time. "Lieutenant Kaiser sent me the guest list and the notes you took at the party."

"Fine. I don't have much to add."

"Were you close to the victim?"

"I'd never met her before. I was writing up the party as a favor to a friend. And I'm not sure Andi is a victim."

"She just *happened* to fall overboard?"

"I don't know. I was at dinner when the ship owner announced we should start eating and not wait for her. I went to look for her and her husband told me she was off crying about the dead lovebirds. But I was on my way to the bridge and I felt it was more important that the Captain calm down the passengers."

"You have nothing more to tell me?"

"At the moment, no."

He closed the manila folder on his desk. "Go home, Hallie. I hear you have a new baby. You're a mother now. A young life is depending on you. You have no business working on a homicide."

"And you, Detective Baer," she said sweetly, "haven't changed a bit."

— Chapter 31 —

SUNDAY AFTERNOON'S TRIP to the ship was not helpful. The police had sealed off all the rooms and cabins with yellow tape, except for the main ballroom which served as a temporary center for lab equipment and everything else.

Hallie arrived just in time to rescue two dead birds from the compost bags in the refrigerator. No, the police hadn't planned to autopsy the doves, but a quick call to Lieutenant Kaiser gave Hallie permission to remove the carcasses.

"Keep the bodies in your fridge, Hallie, not your freezer," she ordered. "I'll call the State Vet tomorrow to schedule a bird autopsy."

Shortly after 8 a.m. Monday, Hallie appeared at the *Golden Gate Star* office to begin her editorial chores. Tulip was already there, greeted her with a professional handshake, then showed her to the former editor's desk.

"Ellen offered to stay and break you in," she said, "but she wanted double salary to do it. I told her that was blackmail and kicked her out."

"You do remember, don't you, Tulip, that I'm only here temporarily? I assume you're still looking for a permanent editor."

"Nothing's permanent," Tulip smiled. "But I do understand our agreement, and that you'll be working half a day until I find someone. I appreciate that you're here. Gloria Barnes, our office manager, is right next door. She'll help with anything you need. How long can you stay today?"

"I told the nanny I'd be home between twelve and one. I assume Ellen had a list of the December features?"

"Yes. She was pissed when she left, so I grabbed her computer to make sure she didn't erase anything. It's all there, Hallie. Have fun. I'm counting on you."

PART 6

— Chapter 32 —

"WHO'S BEEN FUCKING with my coffee pot?" yelled an angry voice from the hall. A woman stormed into the editor's office holding up a steaming mug. "Whoops!"

Seeing Hallie, she quickly covered her mouth. "I'm so sorry! I forgot Ellen's gone. I just got to work, and my coffee tastes like —"

"That's okay. You're Gloria?"

"Yup. You're the new editor?"

"*Temporary* editor. I'm Hallie." She stood and offered her hand. "I'm afraid I'll need help getting started. Would you have some time this morning?"

"My pleasure. I worked closely with Ellen."

The office manager looked to be in her mid-forties. A mop of reddish-brown curls framed a round, freckled face with a wanting-to-please expression. Clearly overweight, she wore a blousy print top over a matching skirt, and dark loafers.

Not waiting to be asked, she pulled up a chair next to Hallie and logged on to the *Star's* website. A few clicks, and the December "Contents" page appeared.

"You should know about our writers," she said, highlighting a name. "They're a talented group, creative but kooky. That's Mary-Carol. She signs everything 'Kiss-kiss' and keeps sending stories we rarely use. This last one wasn't bad, so we're running it, but Ellen had to do heavy editing. Mary-Carol's gonna bitch, so be prepared.

"Then there's Chandra, who runs a flattering author's picture of herself twenty years ago, and wonders why young guys keep calling for dates. Tony's a tax attorney who can't keep himself out of his stories."

"Why should he?"

"Because 'I,' 'me,' and 'my' don't belong in an article. Even worse is when the author uses his own name, as in, 'So he said to me, 'Tony…' ' "

"Why is that so bad?"

"The story's about the story, not the author. Exceptions would be a first person opinion piece or a tale of the author's own experience. Getting back to writers, we mustn't forget Deborah, who knows all the gossip in town and where all the bodies are buried – forgive cliché – but she can't be bothered getting her facts straight so we have to check everything…twice."

"Clarissa," she went on, "interviewed this philanthropist – Klaus something – and developed a mad crush on him. He sent us some pictures he wants back, and she insists on returning them in person."

"Good Lord!" exclaimed Hallie, "how can I possibly remember any of that? I thought I'd just be editing copy."

Gloria laughed. "Well, darlin', it helps to know the personalities you're dealing with. But don't worry about remembering stuff. If you want, I'll get my iPad and work in here for a while."

Hallie relaxed into a smile. "I'd be grateful," she said. "It's a bit overwhelming."

— Chapter 33 —

THE MORNING WENT QUICKLY, as Hallie met her new

colleagues: the advertising sales force, the accountant, the photo editor, the production staff, and Tulip's "right hand," the assistant publisher.

After answering the phone several times, Hallie learned not to take calls from anyone caller I.D. couldn't identify. The writers communicated mostly by email, and she sent out several dozen notices saying that Ellen was gone and she was merely "a temp."

At half past noon, when most of the staff was at lunch, she decided to explore the premises, and was surprised to open the closet in her office and find a large, dusty, file cabinet. In it were photos dating back to 1985, when the magazine was founded as a two-page Richmond District newsletter.

By the time Tulip bought the *Star*, five years later, the paper had grown to six pages, the neighborhood had expanded to include upscale Presidio and Pacific Heights – and a few pictures were even starting to come in digitally.

Her curiosity piqued, Hallie began leafing through the old files, sorted chronologically and by family names, until she came to "Marsh." Snapshots of her parents at various social events in the late '80s and '90s delighted her. After R. Stuart Marsh's death in 1998, there were only a few pictures of Edith Marsh.

One color glossy of her parents was particularly lovely, she thought, showing off her mother's striking white hair and her late father's sweet smile. Surely no one would object if she had it copied for Mumsy, and quietly returned it.

On her way home, after a frustrating morning trying to remember everything, she took the print to a photo shop to be restored and enlarged.

— Chapter 34 —

THAT AFTERNOON, a request from Detective TB sent Hallie driving back to the Hall of Justice to deliver a plastic bag containing two dead doves.

"Thanks," said TB, taking the package from behind his desk. He didn't stand, or offer his guest a chair. "Give me a call in a few days and I'll let you know if the vet finds anything of interest."

Ignoring his rudeness, she asked, "Will they do a full autopsy on the birds?"

"How do I know? I suppose it was your idea to save the bloody carcasses."

"Lieutenant Kaiser and I discussed it," she said, reminding him that she and his Supervisor were good friends. "She wants to know the results, too."

Her not-so-subtle strategy worked. "All right," he said resignedly, "here's the story. We're hoping that a preliminary autopsy will show that the birds died of heat suffocation. That's costing us a hundred bucks. If there's a question, the vet will need tissue sampling and a tox screen. That boosts the price tag way up, and it's not in our budget."

"What if it's important?"

"You want to pay for it?"

"How much?"

"Four hundred."

"I'll give you a check. If you need those tests, please order them."

"Oh, hell, Hallie," he sighed, warming up a bit. "That's nice of you but let's wait and see."

"I'm making my check out to the SFPD," she said, writing away. "Are you through questioning all the guests?"

"I sure as hell hope so. We not only interviewed everyone who was on the ship, but just about everyone Andi knew *off* the ship, from the gal who cut her toenails to the guy who streaked her hair. She wasn't well-liked, but she was generous to those who worked for her, so they'll miss her. To my knowledge, she left almost everything to charity. No one person benefits from her death except her daughter. We're trying to reach her in Europe."

"Could Andi still be alive?"

"Doubtful. Unless the kidnappers she always dreaded had a boat, snatched her off the deck and spirited her away in the dead of night."

"Thanks, TB." She set the check on his desk. "I'll wait to hear from you."

Later that evening, Hallie was holding baby Danny and watching Agatha Christie's *Poirot*, when a voice said, "We interrupt this program to bring you a special bulletin: a body, presumed to be that of missing heiress Alexandra 'Andi' Douvier, has been recovered from San Francisco Bay. No further information is available at this time."

— Chapter 35 —

MONDAY'S LATE NIGHT NEWS had a few more details, and Tuesday's *Chronicle* carried a front-page box:

"At 8:10 p.m. Monday (11/5/12), members of the San Francisco Police Department's Marine Unit recovered the body of 52-year-old Alexandra "Andi" Douvier from the Bay near Angel Island.

"Officer Frank Diaz and his team of two former Marines and one ex-Navy officer, all trained in aquatic rescue techniques, recognized the cadaver from photos. They estimate her approximate TOD (time of death) was 48 hours prior, which matched the victim's reported time of disappearance. Fingerprints confirmed her identity.

" 'We're treating this as a homicide,' Diaz said, 'but we won't be 100 percent certain until we do further investigation and release the body to the Chief Medical Examiner for autopsy.' "

" 'Early signs,' he went on, 'suggest that Ms. Douvier died about ten seconds after hitting the Bay. Although the usual water temperature is 54-60°, the night of 11/3/12 was a chilly 51°. Air temperature was slightly warmer, hovering in the mid-50s with moderate 10 mph winds, indicating that the victim might have been walking on deck.'

" 'The fact that her body did not sink,' " added Diaz, 'raises the possibility that death may have come from a source other than drowning. Sudden cardiac arrest is not uncommon when individuals become abruptly and unexpectedly submersed in icy water.' "

A later edition followed the SFPD (San Francisco Police Department) report, delving into Andi's family history, filling half a page with pictures from social and charitable events over the years.

The writer mentioned the Douvier family's wide-ranging support of causes and institutions, and quoted Andi's grieving husband, Nick Demetropoulos, her best friend, Megin Dixon, and half a dozen community leaders who knew and praised her highly.

A separate obit listed Andi's Swiss Finishing School (now closed), marital history, private clubs, favorite philan-thropies, priceless jade collection, and only blood relative, her 22-year-old daughter, Leah Pipkin, thought to be living in Europe.

The obit ended: *"In lieu of flowers, donations to the Asian Art Museum of San Francisco, 200 Larkin St., SF 94102, or your favorite charity, will be greatly appreciated. Services will be private."*

— Chapter 36 —

AFTER SPENDING THE MORNING at the *Golden Gate Star* proofing, fact-checking, dealing with writers, planning the January issue, and making sure Tulip was still interviewing possible editors, Hallie went home, to find a message from Detective Baer.

She called back right away.

"We have the vet's report on the dead birds," he said. "It's classified, but if you stop by my office around three today, I'll fill you in."

"Thanks, TB, that's nice of you."

"Thank Lieutenant Kaiser," he snapped and clicked off.

"The preliminary report showed no signs of heat exposure," were TB's first words when Hallie walked into his office. "Also, there was no evidence of trauma from being startled or confused by the crowd. The vet hoped he wouldn't need a tox screen, but the birds' stomachs were full, so he had to send food and tissue samples to the lab. Your check was well spent. The birds were poisoned."

"Poisoned?" she gasped, sinking into a chair. "With what?"

He smiled. "Even you won't guess this one. First, you need to know that their feathers protect them from cold and keep their bodies at a high temperature, so the 80° heat would not have been lethal."

"What then? Arsenic? Cyanide?"

"Chocolate."

Seeing her widened eyes, he couldn't resist adding, "Personally, I love a good Hershey bar."

Her frown communicated.

"Okay, so what the vet tells me is that tiny bits of semisweet chocolate, high in sugar and saturated fat, attacked the creatures' sensitive digestive systems, probably causing vomiting and diarrhea. Since the condition wasn't noted or treated, it got worse, hitting the birds' central nervous system and triggering seizures – which apparently, the guests were too busy drinking and stuffing their faces to notice."

"You're telling me that chocolate was the COD of all the birds?"

"No question. Cause of Death was chopped-up chocolate bits someone mixed in with the bird seed."

"Wow! Who had access to the seed?"

"Who didn't? The head hostess had instructions to feed the doves before setting out the cages, so she left the sack of bird food on the galley counter to remind herself."

"Where anyone could've seen it and tampered with it. Who put the seed in the cages?"

"The hostesses and the waiters, who had no way of knowing the mixture was lethal." The detective scratched his head. "Why would anyone want to kill ten pairs of doves?"

"Beats me," Hallie replied. "It might be a crew member with a grudge who wanted to sabotage the party. Maybe a fanatic pet lover who thought death would be better than captivity? I give up – do you see any connection with Andi?"

"No, at least not yet. And Hallie, you must promise you won't mention a word about the vet's report to anybody – not your husband, not your lover, not your closest friend!"

"That's an easy promise to make," she grinned. "They're all the same person."

— Chapter 37 —

WEDNESDAY MORNING, Hallie attended an editorial meeting where the *Golden Gate Star* staff tossed around themes and story ideas for future issues. Those present, including Tulip, agreed with Hallie's request to delete her write-up of Andi's party. They also decided to spike any pictures of the event, since it was beginning to look like the scene of a homicide.

Although she was feeling less stressed in the office, Hallie missed being with Danny, and was pleased to learn that Tulip was interviewing two would-be editors that afternoon.

Danny was asleep in his crib when his mother entered his room, then tiptoed out.

Feeling tired, Hallie lay down on her bed, and began reliving Andi's party in her mind. What puzzled her most was the lack of motives. So many people depended on Andi's patronage and largesse. They would feel a heavy loss in their bank accounts, and were barely worth questioning.

Nick, she knew, would be well taken care of, but not in the grand style he was used to. Andi had given him a luxurious life and almost unlimited freedom; what could he gain from her death?

And there was Megin – would she benefit? From all reports, she was devoted to her friend. In a sense, Andi was her identity and her entrée into a different world. She opened doors for Megin, took her on private jets to Europe, treated her to exclusive spas, provided a car, a designer wardrobe, opera tickets, party invitations and more. Without Andi's prestige and connections, the invitations would disappear as fast as the perks.

Yet Megin seemed to have no illusions about her own social standing, or that she would have anything to offer those in Andi's exclusive strata. She couldn't give grand parties or make major donations. She hadn't a big name. Would Babe de Baubery give a hoot about a middle-class ex-attorney married to a sweet but rather dull law professor?

"Damn," Hallie said to herself, "There must be *some-one* out there who wanted Andi dead."

— Chapter 38 —

ARRIVING AT THE *STAR* office early Thursday morning, Hallie returned her parents' picture to the file where she'd found it, then sat down at her desk to admire the copy she'd just picked up.

Enlarged and photo-shopped, the 8" by 10" glossy showed her formally-dressed parents walking hand-in-hand into the Palace Hotel. The caption on the original photo read: Tuesday, December 23rd, 1997: the annual Debutante Cotillion Ball.

Curious spectators watching the "swells" pass by were a blur in the early picture, but remarkably clear in the enlargement. Even the tiny pink beads on her mother's gown stood out. Mumsy, she thought happily, will be thrilled.

Tulip Rosenkrantz arrived at the *Star* around 10 a.m., relayed the welcome news that she'd hired an editor, and thanked Hallie for her help.

Relieved that her good-deed stint was up, Hallie declined payment, but would be "endlessly grateful" for a cover story on St. Anthony's or the death-with-dignity organization, Compassion & Choices, or both. Done.

Before delving into her email, Hallie made the call that she'd been planning. Nate Garchik, a principal at the prestigious law firm of Garchik, Dooley & Bechtle LLC, was a friend from a recent case she'd helped solve, involving the murder of his fiancée.

"What a nice surprise," said the attorney, answering his direct line. "I'm glad you've got my number, so to speak. How goes it, Hallie?"

"Wonderful, Nate. I've a new baby boy and a new case."

"Congratulations to you and Cas. Tell me more."

"It's not exactly *my* case. You've been reading about Andi Douvier?"

"Who hasn't? My colleague Kevin Dooley is the estate attorney."

"Has he read the will yet?"

"Yes and no." Nate laughed. "That's only in the movies, where they sit around the lawyer's desk and wait to hear who gets what. It dates back to the days when attorneys had to gather families and read the will out loud because so many people were illiterate."

"Oh, sorry. What do they do today?"

"Ms. Douvier – Andi – had a revocable living trust. So Kevin, the trustee/executor, had to determine who was entitled to see the will – usually the accountant and the beneficiaries – and send them copies. I could find out a bit more if you honor the confidentiality."

"I promise! May I call you later?"

"I've a heavy schedule, Hallie. Give me a day or three."

"Will do. Dare I ask about your love life?"

"That torch I'm carrying for Carlie still weighs a ton. But thanks for asking. Call me Tuesday."

PART 7

— Chapter 39 —

THE *CHRONICLE* GAVE the Douvier case full coverage. Monday's paper carried word that the Medical Examiner had begun the autopsy, and that Nick Demetropoulos had given in to media pressure, and released the information everyone was waiting for.

Leaving himself out of the financial picture, he told the reporter that Andi's estate was valued at approximately $500 million. A large sum went to the Wounded Warrior Project to build a veterans' hospital, as Nick had requested. Thirty-six nonprofits enjoyed generous bequests, along with various individuals who had been in her employ.

A mere $1 million went to her daughter, Leah Pipkin, found living in Italy. Leah's refusal to have any contact with her mother, even as an adult, had deeply hurt Andi.

A surprise call woke Hallie from an afternoon nap.

"It's Nate Garchik. Am I disturbing you?"

"Not at all," she said, stifling a yawn. "Danny kept me up half the night, but I'm pleased to hear from you."

"I don't have much, Hallie, but I did find out that Andi's daughter won't be here for the Memorial service. She told my colleague, Kevin Dooley, that she wants nothing to do with her mother's possessions, doesn't want her scrapbooks or anything in the house. She works for some nonprofit organization for the homeless, so he should just send her the money."

"Such bitterness! I wonder what happened?"

"Can I trust you?"

"You know you can, Nate."

"I do. It seems daughter Leah got herself pregnant at the tender age of fifteen. Leah didn't want the baby, and Andi wouldn't consent to an abortion, so the kid ran away and got a Mexican abortion that almost killed her. After that, she never had anything more to do with her mother. Apparently Andi went looking for her a few years ago, but Leah was living her own life and had no desire to reconnect."

"Do we know Leah's last name?"

"She goes by Leah Pipkin Sykes now, so I assume she has a partner, although she's never married. That's about it. Oh, and Nick Demetropoulos neglected to tell the *Chronicle* that he and Megin Dixon each got $5 million cash, plus trusts that support them for life."

"Zowie! Doesn't that make them suspects?"

"Not necessarily. Kevin Dooley swears that neither of them knew about it beforehand. Andi was apparently so hyper about being abducted or killed for her money, she didn't want to give anyone a motive."

"Who inherits her house and the grounds? That property must be worth zillions."

"Kevin said they were still working on that, making sure everything was legal."

"Hmm. It gets more and more puzzling."

"If anyone can put the pieces together…my dime's on you, Hallie."

— **Chapter 40** —

PATIENCE WAS A VIRTUE almost unknown to Hallie Marsh,

and she readily admitted it. Happy to be free of her editorial responsibilities, she planned to spend Tuesday morning playing with Danny, paying bills and catching up on household chores, but her mind had its own agenda.

What would Andi's autopsy show? Would it confirm that she was murdered? What was the exact cause of death? Was she drunk? On drugs? So many questions pounded her brain, but she resisted calling the Medical Examiner, Dr. Thomas Toy.

He was a friend, in a way. At least she considered him a friend, knowing he probably considered her a pest. He was nicer to her than Detective TB, however, and had always been helpful in the past.

Rather than bother him in the midst of an autopsy, she decided to call Helen Kaiser for news about the investigation. The Lieutenant was swamped, but Hallie could come in the next day for a short briefing.

Relieved to have Helen's confidence and trust, Hallie put aside her curiosity and took a moment to stop and remind herself, as she often did, how lucky she was to be alive and healthy, after having had breast cancer.

Giving birth to Danny had been another miracle, and although she didn't consider herself religious, she needed to feel grateful to something – to God – to Nature – or to whatever force created the marvel of the human body.

Then, having spent her allotted three minutes of gratitude, she bundled up her son, strapped him into his car seat, and drove down the hills to the Palace of Fine Arts lagoon. The prospect of introducing Danny to the beautiful swans – and vice versa – delighted her.

Chapter 41

WEDNESDAY at 2 p.m. on the dot, Hallie rapped on Helen Kaiser's door.

"Come in, I'm talking."

Hallie entered and took a seat while the Lieutenant finished her phone call.

"That was Dr. Toy," she said, seconds later, clicking off. "We have a preliminary forensic autopsy and many unanswered questions. We'll know more when they get the tox screen."

"Have you talked to the family?"

"Nick will be here at 4. He wanted a private clinical autopsy, but I told him Dr. Toy is one of the best forensic pathologists in the country. Nick wants to preserve all of Andi's organs, as well as tissue and fluid samples."

"He doesn't trust the M.E.?"

"His lawyer doesn't trust anyone. In a high profile case with millions at stake – almost anything can happen."

"And probably will." Hallie gave a sigh. "What did the autopsy show?"

"For one thing, traces of vomitus in Andi's mouth. That usually means the victim was drowned while alive, but Dr. Toy says she was retching before she was attacked, and didn't die of drowning."

"What did she die of?"

"The official COD is sudden cardiac arrest – her heart stopped when she hit the freezing cold water. Neck bruises indicate that someone tried to shove her into the bay while she was vomiting. When that didn't work, the perp struck her. If she hadn't hit the water, she probably would've died anyway, from blunt force trauma to the head."

"What was she hit with?"

"They found particles of wood in her scalp. We assume that the weapon, whatever it was, was tossed overboard."

"Any footprints?"

"None. The crew swabbed the deck while the caterers were serving dessert."

Hallie looked confused. "So someone hit her on the head and pushed her over the railing –"

"Not exactly. Witnesses say Andi felt sick in the dining room just as they were sitting down to dinner, and excused herself to walk on deck. She didn't want anyone to go with her, not even Megin."

"She must have really felt awful."

"We found Andi's prints on the chain across the gangway," Helen Kaiser continued. "Apparently, she tried to detach the chain so she could heave directly into the water, but she couldn't budge it. So she crouched down under and spilled her guts into the bay. I assume she was trying not to vomit on the deck, and also, she didn't want to be seen."

"Understandable."

"But she was seen. Someone came up behind her, surprised her, tried to push her, and she fought back – hard. There were defensive bruises on her wrists and fingers, and a broken fingernail. Nothing was found under her nails, no skin or fabric threads."

"The perp must have been strong. A man?"

The Lieutenant shrugged. "Andi's personal trainer

85

told us she weighed 102 pounds. Her arm muscles were strong, but she didn't know how to fight. In her drunk and drugged state, almost anyone could have overpowered her."

"Could she have been saved?"

"Dr. Toy didn't think so, not after she'd been struck. Apparently, she began to hemorrhage, indicating her heart was still beating until she hit the water."

"Do we know time of death?" Hallie asked.

"From the tides, winds, water temperature, when and where the body was found, we estimate TOD between 8:45 and 9 p.m."

"What about rigor?"

"Postmortem rigidity was retarded due to the cold water, but began to set in after midnight. It was almost gone when the officers found the body the next night."

The Lieutenant paused for breath. "Dr. Toy explained that after a violent struggle, victims' hands and arms some-times stay stiff – he called it 'cadaveric spasm.' "

"Andi's arms were stiff."

"Yes. That's all I have for you right now. What's that sticking out of your purse? Something for me?"

"Not really." Hallie smiled and extracted a manila envelope. "It's a picture of my parents taken fifteen years ago. I'm going to drop by and surprise Mom with it."

The Lieutenant glanced at the photo. "What a lovely couple! Your mother will be thrilled." She started to put it back, then suddenly stopped. "Wait – that man," she said, pointing. "Do you know him?"

Hallie peered over her shoulder. "Just a face in the crowd."

"He looks familiar…I know I've seen him. May I make a copy of this?"

"Be my guest," Hallie smiled. "I'll trade you for a copy of the autopsy report."

— Chapter 42 —

THE MOMENT she was back in her car, Hallie opened Dr. Toy's official document. The first words she read were:

"There are no autopsy findings pathognomonic of drowning. Therefore, the theory that the victim was alive, and suffered sudden cardiac arrest seconds after hitting the water, remains impossible to prove.

"Nevertheless, excluding the possibility of natural and other causes of death, it may be possible to make an assumption, with the understanding that the diagnosis will be based on exclusion."

After a quick search on her iPhone to translate "pathognomonic" to "characteristic," Hallie realized that Dr. Toy's dissertation was simply self-protective.

Further reading revealed that Andi had a "well-cared-for" exterior, twelve-year-old breast implants, and no signs of recent sexual activity or semen in the vagina.

Her nasal septum, the thin membrane that divides the nostrils, however, showed signs of cocaine use. Her liver was somewhat enlarged, and precancerous polyps showed up in her colon.

Minimal stomach contents indicated that she hadn't eaten dinner, and minimal water in her gut confirmed suspicions of rapid death at the moment of submersion. Urine test and toxicology screen results would tell more.

— Chapter 43 —

THE ANTICIPATED PHONE CALL came Friday, two mornings later. "This is Detective Baer from the Homicide Detail," said a formal-sounding voice. "Is Mrs. Casserly there?"

How irritating, she thought. He's pretending not to know my voice. "This is Mrs. Casserly, better known as Hallie Marsh, TB," she said pleasantly.

"Oh hello, Hallie, it didn't sound like you. The Lieutenant wanted me to tell you the urine and toxicology tests came back."

"And?"

"No surprises. The tox screen showed an elevated blood alcohol level, probably higher before it became diluted. And the victim tested positive for cocaine."

"A lot?"

"No – well, enough. Her husband told Lieutenant Kaiser that she'd agreed to start rehab on Monday. I guess she thought this was her last chance for a coke fix."

"What else did they find?"

"Diphenylmethane, an ingredient in laxative. Also, enamel erosion on her upper and lower bicuspids. She was bulimic. And Ironically, she was something of a health nut – took large numbers of vitamins, Chinese herbs and strange supplements. All we're sure of right now is that the legal determination of the COD confirms foul play. In other words, Andi's official cause of death is sudden cardiac arrest

– SCA – caused by the blunt force trauma that sent her into the freezing water."

"She didn't die of drowning."

"No," said the detective. "And I've a question. The pictures of Andi at the start of the party show that she wasn't wearing jewelry. But a pearl necklace was found on her body. Does that make any sense?"

"Under or outside her jumpsuit?"

"Around her neck. Outside."

"That's strange. Could I see photos of the body when it was found?"

"Yes, drop by the office. This case has us stumped at the moment, Hallie, and I'm forced to confess – I'm even admitting – we could use your help."

"That's quite a confession," she said, laughing.

"The Lieutenant seems to think the social scene is your bailiwick. You know all the players and their family secrets. So go ahead, do your usual snooping thing, but be discreet, keep in touch. And Hallie, remember there's a killer out there who doesn't want to be found. Don't do anything foolish."

— Chapter 44 —

"ANDI'S MEMORIAL SERVICE will be at 10 a.m. tomorrow, 11/19," Helen Kaiser told Hallie Monday morning. She had come to the Lieutenant's office to pick up the photos.

"Where will it be?"

"*Chez* Douvier – a private ceremony at her home for

family and a few friends."

"Wish I could be a fly – well, maybe a butterfly – on the wall," Hallie said. "Is there a guest list? Are you going?"

"Yes and yes. Meg and Nick are allowing police presence for security. They're adamant about no press."

"So now it's 'Meg'? And everything's 'Meg and Nick'? You don't suppose…?"

"Oh, I do suppose. I supposed at the very beginning. Yesterday, I asked Meg, 'Now that Nick's free, will you divorce your husband and marry him?' She looked at me with a straight face, and said, 'Nick couldn't keep his pants zipped long enough to say *I do*.' "

Helen chuckled, then suddenly stiffened, realizing she'd stepped out of her policewoman persona. "I didn't tell you that, right?"

The Lieutenant reached across her desk. "Here are the pix you wanted. You can see Andi's not wearing a necklace when she's greeting her guests. Even if she wore the pearls under her jumpsuit, those large beads would have shown through. Why would she add the necklace later? Those pearls with the diamond clasp are worth at least six figures."

Hallie stared with interest. "Any prints?"

"No – washed away."

"Where's the necklace now?"

"Locked in the evidence box."

"Why didn't the killer take it? And what about Meg and Nick as suspects?"

"Motives?"

"Maybe they're madly in love and somehow found out about Andi's will," Hallie persisted. "They'd have ten million reasons to merge bank accounts. But I agree they're not likely suspects, unless they hired someone. Megin was sitting with nine guests who said she never left the table. And Andi's loving husband was hitting on me at the time of the murder."

"Lucky, you. Bye, bye, Hallie." The Lieutenant pointed to a pile of folders. "I've got thirty other cases to solve."

— Chapter 45 —

Twenty minutes later, Edith Marsh was reading the morning paper at her breakfast table when Hallie walked in and kissed her forehead.

"Hi, Mumsy, your wayward daughter has returned." She grinned and took a seat. "I brought you something."

"You brought me you, darling," beamed Edith, setting down the paper. "That's the best present. Is everything all right? How's my grandson?"

"Danny was just asking about you. You haven't seen him all week."

"I know, dear, forgive me. I've been so busy with the Museum. Have you had breakfast?"

"Yes, thanks." She handed her the manila envelope. "I found this in an old file cabinet at the *Golden Gate Star*."

"What is it?" Edith pulled out the picture and held it up to the sunlight. "Oh mercy, I remember that night," she said softly, as tears filled her eyes. "Your father didn't want to go. The Cotillion started late and he was tired. But I dragged him. The Crockers' granddaughter was coming out and we were sitting at their table."

"You'd never know Dad was unhappy from that picture."

"He was a good sport, even-tempered, like his daughter. And we had a nice evening. Say – who's this man peeking over that woman's shoulder?"

"What man? – Oh! My friend at the police station thought he looked familiar, too. I have no idea."

"No matter, it's a wonderful picture and I'll have it framed for my wall. Any news about Andi?"

"Not really. What are your friends saying?"

"Just how horrible it is. With all her foibles, Andi was well-liked. She almost never turned down a donation request."

Edith shook her head as she stared through her window. "It looks so peaceful out there – on the Bay. Hard to believe she was murdered…"

"Mom – I know you don't approve but I'm really into helping find Andi's killer. When you go to parties and such, will you keep your eyes and ears open for me?"

Her mother's face lit up. "You can keep them open for yourself. Babe de Baubery's having a party on the thirtieth, a week from Friday, and my friend Stewart's going fishing. Why don't you be my escort?"

"I don't know those people. They're your generation, not mine."

"Nonsense. You've met them at my parties. Grimaldi's driving. We'll pick you up at 7:30. Black tie, so wear that pretty Saint Laurent I brought you from Paris."

Hallie hesitated. Much as she looked forward to quiet weekends at home, this was a chance to see many of Andi's "old guard" guests in a different setting. Instinct told her the killer would be there, somewhere, quietly gloating to himself – or herself. It was an opportunity she couldn't resist.

"Okay, thanks, Mumsy. It's a date."

PART 8

— Chapter 46 —

DRIVING HOME from her mother's house, Hallie's thoughts drifted back to her childhood. She was only two years old in 1978, when her parents moved from an apartment on Clay Street to a mansion on upper Broadway, San Francisco's so-called "Gold Coast."

The famous three-block section boasted a stream of multi-million dollar homes. One of them, built by famed architect Willis Polk, was a Georgian manor with four stories of red brick respectability.

Spanning two lots, the structure had views in almost every room, including the three-car garage and English Garden. An indoor swimming pool boasted a retractable ceiling for rare sunny days.

Built in 1920 at a cost of $40,000, Edith and R. Stuart Marsh had acquired it for $3.7 million in 1978. At the height of the dot-com explosion in the late 1900's, Edith turned down an unsolicited offer of $14 million. Her home was not for sale at any price.

Material wealth had never been important to Hallie. She knew that her late grandparents, Zina and Pritchard Doty, had been cattle ranchers and landowners in Montana. Her mother had learned how to rope a steer, shear sheep, and do almost everything the hired hands did. Watching a cow give birth had inspired her to want to become a veterinarian.

The Dotys had encouraged their daughter's ambition. Their property covered 30,000 acres of fields and pastures, and they very much wanted Edith and her two sisters to live and rear their children on family land.

Two-thirds of their wish came true. Edith's sisters married, and dutifully brought their husbands back to the farm. Papa Doty built them homes on the property where they could live independently, but still work for the family.

Edith, alas, disappointed him. She fell in love with Bobby Marsh, an art history major she met at a party. When he proposed, she dropped out of veterinary school. They wed in 1970, and moved to Berkeley, California, where he had a teaching offer.

Not long after, both of Edith's parents died, leaving their assets, in equal amounts, to their three daughters. Edith sold her shares to her sisters, ending up with a generous dowry.

R. Stuart Marsh – a more fitting name, he felt – lost no time investing his wife's inheritance in as many French Impressionist paintings as $12 million would buy. He bounced around art galleries for several years, earned a reputation as collector and connoisseur, and eventually became curator of the de Young Museum.

After his death in 1998, the sale of a single Edouard Manet allowed his widow, Edith Marsh, to become a generous benefactor of the arts.

— Chapter 47 —

GROWING UP the daughter of the wealthy Marshes, Hallie knew that she was privileged, which sometimes set her apart from her classmates. She would often invite friends to a movie, rather than have them see the mansion where she lived.

Her formal schooling ended in 1996 with a bachelor's degree and a master's in education from Smith College. While she was job-hunting, her mother suggested she do volunteer work for the Museum of Modern Art.

To everyone's surprise, Hallie was successful at helping publicize events. Spotting her ability, a board member recruited her to join his PR firm in New York.

After six years in Manhattan, Hallie came home and opened her own PR office – much to Edith's displeasure. Her daughter didn't need to work. But Hallie had always taken her mother's domineering nature in stride, often giving in, then doing whatever she pleased.

Not so her younger brother Rob, who resented Mumsy's well-meant attempts to involve him in art. Defiant and angry, Rob left home, but years later, returned to the city as a successful jazz guitarist. After marrying a lovely woman, he fathered twin girls, and reunited with his family.

Andi's private Memorial Service took place without incident, Lieutenant Kaiser reported, and Thanksgiving 2012 came and went for Hallie, with little progress in solving Andi Douvier's murder.

Shortly after the holiday, TB returned her phone call to report that the police were swamped with more pressing matters than the death of a "socialite."

The case was still alive, he said, but not top priority.

Even the Mayor's office no longer hounded them. Predictably, the detective told her: "Stop wasting your time. Spend it with your son."

There were moments when she was tempted to let matters lie…but not just yet.

— Chapter 48 —

ON THE EVENING OF FRIDAY, November 30th, Grimaldi, longtime butler, chauffeur, and handyman for the Marsh family, rang Hallie's doorbell. Cas answered with Danny in his arms, waved to Mumsy in the car, and kissed his wife goodbye when she came down the stairs.

"I'll go quickly," she whispered, as Danny reached out for her and started to cry.

Gracing the entrance to her Nob Hill penthouse, the stunning and much-sought-after Countess Babe de Baubery stood smiling, welcoming each of her 200 guests.

Behind her, a towering Christmas tree sparkled with colored lights and dazzling ornaments. Overhead, white pine boughs laced with wired cranberries hung from various chandeliers. Soft sounds of the Gary Zellerbach Trio playing holiday music heightened the festive mood.

To the right of the host, the ubiquitous Wallace Robinson made sure each arrival was relieved of his or her coat, and offered a glass of Crystal champagne or whatever libation was desired. Should the Countess momentarily forget a guest's name, Wallace would quietly provide it.

"How nice that your beautiful daughter could join

us," said the host, greeting Edith.

"Mrs. R. Stuart Marsh, Ms. Hallie Marsh," said Wallace, bowing.

"Yes, of course. Hallie," the Countess echoed. "What a charming frock."

"Thank you," Hallie said. "You look fabulous!"

The moment she said it, she knew it sounded awkward. But the Countess was already onto the next guest.

"She's gorgeous," Hallie whispered to her mother. "And her dress *is* beautiful, isn't it?"

Edith nodded. "She loves Valentino red. I would've chosen something less revealing."

Their chatter was interrupted by an elderly couple who bestowed double-cheek air kisses on Edith, gave limp handshakes to Hallie, made inane comments about the decorations, and moved on.

"Mom," Hallie whispered, "this is going to be a long evening."

— Chapter 49 —

HALF AN HOUR LATER, the party was at its peak, the noise level high, trays of hors d'oeuvres seemed to empty as soon as they were passed. Edith Marsh, deep in conversation with the Museum Director, was unaware that her daughter was checking out the décor, as well as the guests.

The de Bauberys were avid collectors. It didn't seem to matter what they collected as long as they had an impressive supply.

Every surface in their spacious living room held a

cluster of *objets:* Chinese snuff bottles, Lladro figurines, antique inkwells, World War 1 medals, Tibetan Fu Dogs, and some items Hallie couldn't identify.

Most striking was a chinoiserie cabinet, with a shelf of what she recognized as near-priceless Fabergé eggs. If someone immoral enough to kill Andi was there, in the same room, mightn't he or she be tempted by such a display of wealth? And yet, if Andi's killer was money-motivated, why hadn't he taken her pearls?

Wandering into the dining room, Hallie saw a table heavy with platters of crab legs, prawns, lobster, caviar on mini-crêpes, foie gras, sliced filet, and every imaginable kind of dessert from macaroons to mousse. A shoulder tap broke into her observations.

"Hi, Cinderella."

Hallie swung around. The voice belonged to Nick Demetropoulos, predictably handsome in his white dinner jacket. Numbers raced through her brain. Not even a month since Andi died. Wasn't it a bit soon for him to be making the party scene?

"Hello, Mr. D," she said, with as much warmth as she could muster.

"You disappeared the other night and didn't even leave me a glass slipper."

"The other night? You mean the night your wife was murdered?"

"Well, yes, if you want to put it that way. It's been terrible – hard on all of us. I miss Andi constantly, every-where I go, everything I do. But life goes on. You didn't tell me your name."

100

"You didn't ask." She wasn't sure whether to continue or try to escape. "It's Hallie – Hallie Marsh, and my married name is Casserly."

"Fortunate guy. Why are you so hostile?"

"Am I? Sorry. I've been helping the police try to find your wife's killer and we haven't had much luck. Do you have any theories?"

"You bet." He paused to empty his champagne glass. "Andi wasn't murdered. She was dizzy from booze and coke, went out on deck to get sick, slipped, bumped her head against the hull, and fell into the water. It wasn't suicide and it wasn't murder. If you're working with the police, tell them to look for real criminals and to stop wasting their fucking time!"

With a quick, angry glance, he turned and strode away.

— Chapter 50 —

SPEECHLESS, Hallie stared after Nick Demetropoulos just as Wallace Robinson walked over toting a tray of cheese puffs. "Was that poor, inconsolable husband making a play for you?" he asked.

"He's just upset. Doesn't think his wife was murdered. He thinks she hit her head and fell overboard."

"Isn't that possible?"

"As they say, Wallace, anything's possible. But if no one murdered Andi, who murdered the birds?"

"People can be strange, my dear. I've wondered what kind of person could be that cruel, myself. I'd better pass these goodies before they get cold."

Hoisting his tray in the air, he disappeared into the crowd.

Uncomfortable as she was in that elite ambiance, Hallie knew she would have to circulate if she wanted to pick up information. Spotting some of her mothers' friends in the living room, she took a deep breath and walked over to greet them.

To her surprise, her crime-solving reputation preceded her. The women in that small group immediately asked about Andi Douvier. "What did the autopsy show?" "Was she a drug addict?" "Was she killed by someone at the party?" "What are the police doing?"

Hallie answered as well as she could, at the same time trying to learn what Andi's friends were thinking and saying – with little success. Talk soon moved on to who would chair the Opera Ball when Babe stepped down, the Rudolf Nureyev Exhibition at the de Young, and everything from the Mayor's trip to China to the city official whose anti-gay-marriage stance fizzled when he admitted to living with his barber.

Shortly before nine, Edith Marsh was happy to find her daughter chatting and mingling, and Hallie was equally happy that her mother wanted to leave. As soon as they stepped out of the elevator, Edith asked, "Did you notice that couple riding down with us?"

"Sure," said Hallie. "Gorgeous young blonde trophy wife."

"Did you notice her husband with the beard?"
"No. Should I have?"

102

"I thought you might recognize him. Remember that wonderful photo from the Deb Ball you gave me? I'm pretty sure he was that mystery man – you know, the face in the crowd."

"Hmmm," Hallie mumbled. "The plot gets 'curiouser and curiouser.'"

PART 9

Chapter 51

CAS WAS WORK-WEARY and needed a vacation, he told Hallie, so on the tenth of December, 2012, they packed up eight-month-old Danny and his nanny, Jenny, and flew to Honolulu.

A rented house on the beach worked well for them. While Jenny took the baby to play in the sand, his parents walked, slept, shopped, toured the island, and renewed the love they sometimes took for granted in their busy lives.

By the time they were ready to come home, two weeks later, Hallie and Cas felt rested and invigorated. Danny was happy, too, having spent hours trying to pull himself up to a standing position so he could take his first steps. They arrived at the San Francisco airport just in time to rush home and dress for Christmas Eve dinner at Edith's.

The week went fast, Cas returned to work, Hallie helped her mother through minor surgery, and then, on the first Wednesday of 2013, Hallie stopped by the Hall of Justice. The officer on duty alerted Lieutenant Helen Kaiser, who said, "Send her in."

"If it were anyone but you, I'd say I'm too busy." Helen looked up from her desk. "What brings you here?"

"Happy New Year, and I won't stay more than a minute." Hallie's eyes focused on a huge pile of folders. "I can see you're swamped. Any news about Andi?"

"Nothing, sorry to say."

"What about the old picture?"

"Picture? Oh, you mean the photo of that man and your parents. Something came in, but it's in that pile and I haven't had two seconds to look at it."

"When you do, will you let me know?"

"Don't I always, my friend? Now goodbye, thanks for the visit."

— Chapter 52 —

ON A QUIET AFTERNOON, almost a week later, Hallie sat at her computer, checking her emails. One from the SFPD caught her eye:

`   *"Facial Recognitions matches pix to other pix in criminal database. Man in photo is Benedict Billings, suspect in death of wife; body found in foyer of Russian Hill condo, 12/23/97. Case cold — not worth further investigation."*

Hallie stared at Helen Kaiser's message, read it twice, then hit "Reply" and typed, *"No statute of limitations on murder, right? May I see file?"*

The answer came quickly. *"No! Waste of your time & mine."*

`   *"Please?"*

"Billings is respected lawyer — had airtight alibi."

"PLEASE?"

"TB's right. You can be pain in ass. Answer is no. Goodbye!"

Rejection rarely deterred Hallie. Perhaps showing cold case files to non-police personnel was against rules. It took her about four seconds to Google Benedict Billings. She would never have recognized the young, clean-shaven man in the 1997 picture to be the older gent in a recent online photo. The gray moustache and goatee, along with his silvery hair, gave him an altogether different appearance.

Under Billings' name, a *Chronicle* article had a full account of the sudden death of his forty-four-year-old wife, Nina. He was forty-eight in '97, which would make him sixty-four in 2013.

What happened, according to Billings, was that the couple had a fight about his mother-in-law, whom she'd invited to stay with them. He'd offered to pay her hotel bills at the Fairmont, Nina said that would hurt her mother's feelings, and he'd stalked out in a huff. That was about 8 p.m. on the evening of December twenty-third, 1997.

Deciding he needed a drink, Billings drove to the Blue Leaf Bar on Market Street, near his office. Four Martinis later, after a long chat with the bartender, he ordered a fifth Martini.

'Twas the night before Christmas Eve, and the lonely were drowning their sadness in booze. Every bar stool was filled, and the crowd kept growing. Not wanting to see anyone he knew in his inebriated state, Billings grabbed his drink, moved to a dark corner, and soon passed out with his head on the table.

Later, at a private hearing, the bartender swore that Billings was sitting there until 10 p.m. The man remembered because that was when his shift was up and his replacement arrived.

By that time, the witness said, Billings seemed to have sobered enough to drive home. That's when he found Nina's body on the floor and policemen swarming through his house.

Preliminary inspection showed that Nina died from falling against a heavy bronze statue in their foyer. She was slim and petite, and wearing three-inch heels at the time, so it did seem possible that she could have slipped on the marble floor. If not, who would have pushed her?

Three strong suspects emerged: Nina's husband, Benedict Billings, their maid/housekeeper Ellsie Groon, who confirmed that she had recently mopped the floor and it could have been slippery, and the maid's boyfriend, Zack Conner, a waiter at The Burger Bistro.

Both men had firm alibis for their time. Billings was at the Blue Leaf Bar till 10, and Conner was able to prove he was at work all night. Ellsie, the maid, swore she was in her room watching television, and hadn't heard the argument. Her fingerprints were found on the victim's blouse, but Ellsie explained that she had just ironed it, and had helped Mrs. Billings put it on.

Ellsie insisted that she loved her job, was well paid, and had no possible motive. Having previously worked nine years for the Baroness de Baubery, she had a first-class reference.

A fourth option was that someone Nina knew well enough to let in the door had harmed her, but the doorman insisted he'd been on duty all evening and no visitors or strangers had come in.

The police had questioned the other seven tenants in the building. Since it was two days before Christmas, they were either out partying or home preparing for the holiday.

They barely knew Nina and Benedict Billings; socializing among the residents was rare.

As always, according to the newspaper article, the District Attorney had a backup of cases. Billings had a top reputation and a growing practice, the maid's boyfriend had no record or outstanding debts, and both men had proved they weren't anywhere near the scene. The maid had excellent references from top citizens, nothing to gain by killing her employer, and a plush job to lose.

After many weeks, the D.A. released a statement:

"My office has completed an exhaustive investigation of the evidence in this case, and found no grounds to indict any of the suspects, nor have we found conclusive evidence of foul play. The Medical Examiner has ruled the cause of death 'Undetermined.'"

Despite the pleas of Nina's family and friends to keep searching, the case grew cold.

— **Chapter 53** —

THE NEXT DAY, when Hallie returned from a morning walk with Danny, a message from TB awaited her. Pressure to give the Douvier case priority was starting again, he said. Had she heard any more about Andi?

She called back. "We were in Hawaii, TB, and I'm just catching up. I've accepted a ladies' luncheon, which is a pretty good source of gossip. I'm hoping to pick up something. Nothing new on your end?"

"There is something. I don't know if it's connected to the Douvier case or not." He paused to reach for a file.

"After the party, the wine steward on the Medusa noticed that a rare bottle of DRC Pinot Noir was missing from the ship's wine cellar."

"DRC?"

"Domaine de la Romanée-Conti, however you pronounce it. A bottle's worth anywhere from $10k to $100,000. As luck would have it, the steward took inventory that afternoon and the missing wine was there at the time. Two crew members refinished the floor around 4 p.m. It wasn't completely dry, so whoever went in there that evening would have some slight residue on his or her shoes."

"You're going to examine everyone's shoes?"

"Because of the valuable wines, a ship security officer stood at the entrance to the cellar, and had every visitor or crew member sign a sheet before going in. Two of my men are on the ship now, with warrants to search nine cabins, from the First Mate's on down, and check the shoes of those who signed in. If the shoes test positive for varnish residue, as they should, the detectives will search the cabin and bring the shoes back to the lab for more testing."

"More testing?"

"Yes. The crime lab may be able to tell what parts of the room the person visited. The floor was varnished in two parts; the farthest end of the cellar got old varnish until it ran out. The front is new varnish. If someone has only new varnish residue, he couldn't have taken the bottle because the missing wine was in the back."

"I see – process of elimination. What about the caterers? What about guests touring the ship?"

"We've a list of forty-two names, and the security

officer swears no one got by him. It's dark inside, and some-one could easily have slipped the bottle into a large purse or bag. We'll look into everyone on the list."

Hallie blinked. "You're going to the homes of Andi's VIP guests to check the soles of their shoes?"

"Only five couples visited the wine cellar, and yes, we'll check the shoes they wore to Andi's party."

"What a lot of work! What if they give you the wrong shoes?"

"If there's *no* varnish residue, we'll know they're the wrong shoes." TB exhaled quietly. "Look, Hallie, it's just good solid police work. We spend hours and hours on small details that may or may not be a waste of time. If these forty-two people entered the wine cellar, their shoes will show it. And if so, we have warrants – as part of a grand theft investigation – to search their premises for the missing bottle. The only difference is that my men won't tear up their homes and leave a mess like they do on TV."

Hallie paused to plan her words. Her next question was crucial. Then, in as sweet a voice as she could muster, she said, "TB – would you be kind enough to send me the forty-two names?"

— Chapter 54 —

WITH ANDI DOUVIER'S murder still under heavy police in-vestigation, Hallie turned her thoughts to the late Nina Billings. At dinner that night, she told Cas about the case, and wondered if she should visit her psychic friend, Zlotta Kofiszny.

"What for?" asked Cas. "She's a fake and you know it."

"Of course I know it, and she knows I know it. You once told me all psychics are fakes, especially the ones who claim to see the future. But then you saw Zlotta on TV and you said she was a damn good fake – amazingly observant and intuitive. Remember?"

"Ah yes, I remember it well. And you've been to see her once or twice. Has she ever really helped you?"

"She's good at reading people. I could show her the pictures I got off the Internet – Benedict and Nina Billings, the maid and her boyfriend. It can't hurt anything, except my wallet."

Cas laughed. "It's your money, darling. If you want to flush it away, be my guest."

— Chapter 55 —

THE NEXT MORNING, Thursday, after being told that Madame Zlotta had no openings before February, Hallie made an appointment for three and a half weeks later. Then she stopped by to see her mother. Not finding her in one of the usual rooms, Hallie poked her head into the kitchen.

Grimaldi was standing by the black granite island, polishing silver. "Your mother's gone to the Museum, Miss Hallie. May I bring you some coffee?"

"Oh, no thanks, Grims. I'm just wondering – a few weeks ago, I brought over an old picture of her and my Dad taken years ago. Would you have seen it lying around?"

"You mean that lovely photo of her and Mr. Marsh

going to the Cotillion?"

"Yes, exactly! Do you know where it is?"

"I do, indeed. I took it to be framed a few days ago. It's probably ready to be picked up."

"There was a date on the back of the picture. You didn't happen to…?"

"I'm afraid not, Miss Hallie."

"Well, it's sort of important. Is that the same framer she's always used, down on Sutter Street?"

"It is." He smiled. "Cranky old chap, too."

"Well, I'm off to see him. Thanks for the info, and give Mumsy my love."

Twenty minutes later, Hallie slid four quarters into a parking meter and entered an art gallery/frame shop near Union Square. The owner was not happy to see her. Having spent several hours placing the fragile photo in a custom setting, he tried his best to talk her out of ruining his handiwork.

At her insistence, however, along with her offer to double the original price, he begrudgingly slit open the frame, removed the photo and handed it to her.

All Hallie needed was a glance to confirm her suspicion. The date on the back of the picture was December twenty-third, 1997, the same night – and about the same time – that Benedict Billings claimed he was passed out in the Blue Leaf Bar.

— Chapter 56 —

HALLIE SAID NOTHING about her discovery. A man's life and

113

reputation were at stake, and she would need many more facts before contacting the police.

Mumsy was another consideration. Unlike many of her friends, Edith Marsh shunned personal publicity, and would be most distressed if that picture – possibly critical evidence – showed up in print or online. Hallie decided to wait to see Madame Zlotta, then plan how to proceed.

In the meantime, one late afternoon, Hallie followed an impulse to check out the Blue Leaf Bar on Market Street. Inside the dimly lit room, she noted a long counter, shelves of various bottles and mixes against the wall, scattered tables in the rear. The bartender was also the owner, but he'd only had the place three years, and had never heard of Benedict Billings.

Nor had his dozen or so customers. One shaggy-looking gent said he'd been coming there for twenty years, and remembered reading about a murder, but couldn't recall any details.

Hallie wasn't about to give up. After ordering a tomato juice, she began questioning the owner about the bar's history. Surely they had some old scrapbooks – Photographs? Financial records? Anything?

"Sorry, Miss," he said. "I was told all that stuff got thrown away when the bar got retrofitted after the '89 quake."

"Oh, too bad." She was getting nowhere. "Say, the Palace Hotel isn't far from here, right?"

"Not unless you consider a three-minute walk far. D'ya know what that joint gets for a drink now?"

"More than you do, I'll bet."

"Don't get me started." He groaned, and moved away to serve a customer.

Hallie gulped her juice, left a bill on the counter and headed for her car. The trip, she admitted to herself, was a waste of time. She hadn't found any leads, hadn't gotten any answers, and all she'd picked up was a tiny piece of information that might possibly prove helpful if she decided to pursue the case. And at that moment, she no longer doubted that she would.

PART 10

— Chapter 57 —

FEBRUARY FINALLY ARRIVED, bringing warm spring weather as well as red eyes and sneezes from the pollens. Like so many hay fever sufferers, Hallie took antihistamines to quell her symptoms. Sometimes they worked, sometimes they didn't.

On this Monday morning, she had taken a pill, which seemed to be helping her nose, if not her mood. Driving slowly, she pulled up to her destination, trying to control her frustration. Why had Zlotta's assistant made her wait almost a month for an appointment? Was Zlotta really that busy or was it just for show? Having spent twelve years in the PR business, she assumed the latter.

The self-proclaimed "World's Leading Celebrity Psychic" read palms and futures, chatted with the dead, and specialized in dispatching evil spirits. These and other miracles took place in a gray stucco Victorian on Bush Street, midway between Hallie's home in Pacific Heights, and downtown San Francisco.

Zlotta's residence was much as Hallie remembered it, plain and unremarkable, save for a dove of peace under the address plate. The bell was answered almost instantly.

"Welcome back, Sister Hallie," smiled a short, stout man in a black gown. "I'm Rev. Barney of the Church of Serenity. We've been looking forward to seeing you."

"Thanks, I do have an appointment…at last."

"You certainly do. What I meant is that Madame

Zlotta knew you were coming back to us. She said — I think it was last December — that we'd see you in either February or October."

"She was right, as always. You're looking well, Reverend." Her eyes rested momentarily on his hairless head and round, smiling face.

"Thank you, Sister Hallie." He led the way towards a table covered with flyers. "Madame Zlotta will be with you shortly. Your donation to the church will be a hundred and fifty dollars for a thirty-minute reading."

"Wow! That's fifty more than last time."

Ignoring her comment, he went on: "Should you wish the candle ceremony to protect you from negative spirits, it's only fifty dollars."

"No, thanks. Thirty minutes is fine." What a rip-off! Cas would think she was insane.

After returning her credit card, Rev. Barney pushed aside a curtain leading to the Madame's parlor. Thick draperies hid the bright sun. Three candles on a round table provided the only lighting. As before, the scent of incense was strong. Ravel's *Pavane for a Dead Princess* played softly in the background.

The salon looked much more stylish; business must be good. The two purple velvet chairs Hallie remembered had been newly upholstered in a smart salmon-colored fabric. Freshly painted walls echoed the pinks and reds of the faded Persian carpet. The same portrait of a young Madame Zlotta dominated the room, her eyes fixed on the observer. Photos and clips from recent publications competed for space on an oversize poster board.

The patter of feet alerted Hallie – and then, a surprise. The flowery floor-length skirt the psychic had worn at their last session eighteen months earlier, had been replaced by a tailored wool pantsuit. Gone was the red hair band, the dangling gold-hoop earrings, the multi-colored beads, the clumpy Birkenstocks. Even her white hair had been cut short, framing a wrinkled, once-pretty face.

She smiled and offered a hand. "Welcome, my dear. I see you're troubled. May I serve you some tea?"

"No, thanks, Madame Zlotta." The clock was already ticking in her brain. "I'm not troubled, just curious. May I tell you why I'm here?"

— Chapter 58 —

NOT WANTING to leave out any details, Hallie related everything she knew about the Billings incident. "If the lawyer did murder his wife," she concluded, "he should pay for it. If he didn't, his name should be cleared and the guilty person punished. From all I've read, no one really thinks the death was accidental. The case deserves answers, and Nina's family deserves closure, don't you think?"

Zlotta often took sixty or so seconds to answer, which irritated Hallie, though she never dared complain.

Finally the psychic spoke. "Luck is with you, dear child. The spirits have agreed to help you with this problem. Did you bring pictures?"

Hallie opened a folder and placed four small photos on the table.

Zlotta's flashlight lit up the images. She stared for a

long time, running her hand over each one. Then she lowered her voice: "I'm afraid these are useless, my sweet. Copies of newspaper pictures from your computer have traveled too far, through too many incarnations. They have no soul. I need fresh, vital pictures, preferably glossy, and large enough so I can get a true sense of the person."

"These are no use at all?"

"Can you get recent photos?"

"I don't even know where anyone lives."

"Ahhh." Her eyes widened. "You've just begun your search for the truth."

"Yes, I came to you first."

"In that case, let us use our powers of reason." She took Hallie's hand. "If your picture – the one of your beloved parents – shows that Mr. Billings was at the Palace Hotel at the time of the unfortunate death of his wife, does that not prove his innocence?"

"No." Hallie gently pulled her hand away. "When I visited the Blue Leaf Bar, where he was supposed to have fainted, I learned that a person could walk to the Palace Hotel and back in six minutes."

"And that proves…?"

"According to the testimony I read, the bar was dark and crowded the night of the murder. Mr. Billings could've slipped out for some air, stuck his head in the crowd of on-lookers at the hotel, then walked right back to his table in the bar, and passed out again. Apparently, nobody missed him."

"Go on, my sweet."

"It's also true that he could've used that time while

he was out of the bar – to walk to the Palace Hotel, go home and kill his wife, then go back to the bar. Who knows? The picture doesn't prove anything."

"Well, my pretty pet, our time has flown by, and since I could not communicate with the pictures, I will tell you that I am getting strong messages from the spirits. Yes – what is that again?" She cupped her ear. "Find the aid? What is that? Ahh, yes, yes, I see. Thank you, my friends. Blessings on the holy messengers."

She turned to Hallie. "They tell me that you must seek until you find the woman they call the maid. They say that she will have the magic key to the truth. And is there someone named Deb? Maybe Debra or Debby?"

"I can't think of anyone."

"You will, my child, you will. Take home these precious bits of wisdom. Thoughts will flow if you stay open to receive them. May the spirits be with you, my dear."

— Chapter 59 —

THAT EVENING, ten-month-old Danny Casserly was in the living room with his father, taking a step, tumbling, then getting up and trying again.

"He's determined, like his mother," said Cas, as Hallie walked in.

"And stubborn like his father. Don't you want some cake?"

"No, thanks, I have to keep my boyish figure."

"You had three cookies when you came home. I saw the crumbs."

"Always snooping."

Pretending she didn't hear, Hallie walked over to Danny, told him how well he was doing, hugged him and handed him to the nanny. "Thanks, Jenny. I'll be up to tuck him in."

Cas sat down and patted the seat of the couch. "I told you all about my day, sweetheart. How was yours?"

"I went to see Madame Zlotta," she said, sinking into the seat beside him. "And yes, I did overpay, and no, she wasn't much help. She did say the spirits want me to question the Billings' maid, Ellsie, though I couldn't find her in the phone book or on Google. The spirits also asked if I knew someone named Deb or Debra."

"And what did you tell the spirits?"

"I didn't talk to them directly, you understand. But Zlotta's pretty intuitive, as we've discussed, and sometimes she does come up with good leads. I remember reading that Ellsie worked for the de Bauberys' before she went to the Billings'. And I thought maybe that was the clue – de B, Deb?"

"Too far-fetched."

She shrugged. "I can't think of anything else."

"I can. Where were your parents going in that old picture?"

"To the Cotillion."

"What kind of Cotillion?"

"Omigod! The *Deb* Cotillion! Darling, you're brilliant. But what's the connection? What does it mean?"

"Probably nothing, considering the source. But if you

want to find the maid, why don't you ask Mrs. de Baubery?"

"I can't just call up *la Contessa* and ask about someone who worked for her twenty years ago."

"Your mother could ask her."

"What a good idea. I'll call Mumsy right now!" Jumping up, she kissed his cheek, and disappeared down the hall.

— Chapter 60 —

EDITH MARSH WAS NOT a fan of her daughter's crime-solving activities. Nevertheless, after some persuasion, she agreed to call her friend, Babe de Baubery, and invite her for lunch. Her reason for including Hallie, she told the Countess, was that Hallie needed a pep talk on opera – something Babe was always glad to provide.

Two weeks passed. On a quiet Monday in mid-February, all eyes in the elegant dining room of the private Presidio Golf Club turned to stare at a tall, slim, beautiful brunette. Dressed in head-to-toe Oscar de la Renta – overdressed, actually, for a golf club – the woman glanced around the room, seemingly oblivious to the gawkers.

Guesses of her age ranged from fifty to seventy-five. Those in the know recognized Babe de Baubery from her photos; others assumed she was a model or a celebrity.

Head held high, the Countess quickly spotted Edith and Hallie at a table for three, blew kisses, and sat down to join them. "Hello, you darlings. What a lovely spot, Edith!

I didn't know you played golf."

Edith laughed. "At my age? Hardly! We're what they call 'social members.' We use the Club's dining rooms – their chef is superb."

"So nice of you to take your time to meet us, Countess de Baubery," said Hallie.

"*Do* call me Babe, darling. Everyone from my plumber to the Queen of England calls me that. Now Hallie, sweet potato, what's this I hear about your not liking opera?"

"I actually do like –"

The Countess needed no explanation. She launched into a monologue about the virtues of Verdi, Puccini, and Wagner, the historical background of the art, the need for culture among young people, and how her own knowledge and love of opera made her a warmer, more compassionate person.

Happy to let her ramble, Hallie would ask an occasional question and nod her head to show agreement. When their Cobb Salads arrived, however, the Countess turned her attention to check if the bacon was crisp (it was), if the blue cheese dressing was on the side (it was), and if the meat was chicken breast, not turkey, and not dark meat (it was). Thus reassured, the Countess raised her fork.

Hallie saw a chance to switch subjects. "That was a lovely party you had, Babe," she said. "We rode down in the elevator with a Mr. Billings. I remember reading about him years ago."

"Indeed, that poor man. He worshipped that adorable wife of his and people are still cruel enough to think he 'did her in,' as they say. But he's a successful lawyer with a charming new wife, and that tragedy was in the late '90s. Today, everyone accepts the Billings' and they do entertain marvelously."

"And support the opera," added Edith.

"Major donors, no less." The Countess turned to Hallie. "I hear you're quite the female Sherlock Holmes these days. Are you helping find out what happened to our darling Andi?"

"The police are very much on the case and I'm trying to stay out of their hair," she said, smiling. "You're right, though. I'm intrigued by unsolved mysteries. That's why I remember the Billings story so well. Wasn't there something about a maid and her boyfriend?"

"Ellsie Groon. How could you forget that name, poor thing. She worked for us for nine years and then my darling Émile wanted to spend a year in Paris with his sister, who's quite common, I'm afraid, and her husband, who's worse, but what can you do?"

"Umm – what happened to Ellsie when you went to Paris?"

"I found her a job with the Billings. And they absolutely loved her until that dreadful night."

"Any idea where Ellsie is now?"

"Heavens, no. She had a brother, Howard or Harold or something, who drove a limo, I think. Tell me, Edith, what's happening at the Museum?"

Lunch dragged on, until Hallie finally excused herself, promised to attend more operas, and air-kissed the ladies goodbye.

PART 11

— Chapter 61 —

"LIEUTENANT KAISER told me to call you." TB's voice boomed in Hallie's ear. It was shortly after eight the next morning, and she was exhausted from Danny's restless night. "We may have a break in the Douvier case."

"A break?" She sat up in bed. "Tell me!"

"Remember the shoes? Wine cellar on the Medusa – expensive bottle missing? We hoped to find a suspect by examining varnish residues on the soles of forty-two pairs of shoes?"

"I remember. Any luck?"

"Not with the wine. It's still missing. The bad news is that all but one pair of shoes showed residue of the old varnish, indicating that their owners visited the area of the theft. But by the time we could get search warrants for the homes of ten guests, twelve ship personnel and nineteen catering staff, the wine would be long gone."

"Did they examine the shoes for anything else? Signs of a struggle? Blood?"

"They checked the soles, and found fresh saliva, hairs, and one shoe had recent blood. They'll test everything for DNA."

"To see if it matches Andi's?"

"A long shot, but yes."

"Are they doing nuclear testing or mitochondrial?"

"Where the hell did you learn that?"

"Doesn't matter. I hope it's both. Mitochondrial only tests DNA inherited from the mother."

"That's up to the lab guys. All I know is that they're

holding onto the shoes for the moment. Unfortunately, this case has been open for more than three months, and now we have to wait three weeks more for the DNA results."

"But that's great police work, TB. Congratulations!"

"Save your compliments, Hallie. We still know zip."

— Chapter 62 —

WITH ANDI DOUVIER'S CASE on hold for at least another three weeks, Hallie turned her attention back to Nina Billings. Grimaldi, her mother's butler/chauffeur, had no idea of the identity of "Howard or Harold who drove a limo." The man, according to Babe de Baubery, *might* be the brother of her former maid, Ellsie Groon.

As Hallie reminded herself, Ellsie was present in the Billings' house the night Nina Billings was killed, and was still one of three suspects. But the Countess's clue seemed useless. After spending most of the morning Googling and calling limo firms in the Bay Area, she finally found a San Francisco company called "Drivers 4U" that had a "chauffeur" named Howard Janss – not Howard Groon.

Having seen their ads, she knew that the firm supplied people who would drive the clients' own cars to their destination, wait for them, then drive them home. Since no limo was involved, it seemed unlikely that Howard Janss was the man the Countess had in mind. Yet it was worth a stab. Perhaps Janss was Elsie's step-brother, or possibly Ellsie's maiden name.

"We don't give out phone numbers," the dispatcher explained, so Hallie left a message. To her surprise, Howard

Janss returned her call that afternoon.

"Thanks for getting back to me," she said, "I'd better clarify that I'm not calling to hire you, Mr. Janss. I'm trying to find a woman named Ellsie Groon, and I heard that perhaps you could help me."

Instantly defensive, the man asked, "Who told you that?"

"My nanny, Jenny Neilsen," she lied, thinking fast. "She used to work with Ellsie."

"Why do you want to find her?"

"Jenny mentioned that she'd like to see her. I thought I'd surprise her."

"Go to hell," he snapped, and hung up.

Refusing to be discouraged, Hallie told herself that Howard Janss had asked too many questions not to know something. The good news was that her "Caller ID" had recorded his phone number.

Jenny Neilsen was in the bathroom sponging Danny, and laughed when she heard Hallie's story. If it would help catch a killer, she'd be delighted to tell a white lie for her employer.

"Let's wait a few hours," she told Jenny. "Then please, call Mr. Janss and turn on the charm?"

— **Chapter 63** —

JENNY NIELSEN had a way with men, regardless of their age. As a pretty blonde growing up in Norway, she learned that flirting and flattery usually paid off. Now in her fifties, she retained her skills, but they were less effective.

After getting detailed instructions, she held up the phone so Hallie could listen, and entered Howard Janss's number. A man answered.

"*Hei, goddag,*" she said in her best Norwegian.

"*Goddag,*" came the answer. "Who's this?"

"Yenny Nielsen," she singsonged. Hallie restrained a giggle. "You know my friend Ellsie, ya?"

"Ya." Long pause. "Why do you want Ellsie?"

"I always miss her. She was goot friend."

"I'll tell her. She works at a hospital in Napa."

"You give me her phone number, ya?"

"*Dra til Helvete*, he said, and was gone.

— Chapter 64 —

HOWARD JANSS'S FAVORITE SUGGESTION to visit Hades had zero impact on Hallie, even in Nowegian. Excited to learn where Ellsie was working, she searched online, learning that there were two hospitals of note in Napa, a charming county a little over an hour's drive north of San Francisco.

The Queen of the Valley Medical Center was in Napa, and St. Helena Hospital was in St. Helena, a nearby town with a population of 5800.

Hallie had no doubts that Janss was Ellsie's brother, and that he'd let slip the line about the hospital, immediately regretting it. But if Ellsie were innocent of killing Nina Billings, and had no motive and a firm alibi, why was he so intent on protecting her?

The following Monday, Hallie drove to the Queen of the

Valley Medical Center, a large non-profit institution known for its state-of-the-art facilities. The hospital was mostly supported, she learned, by the wealthy Napa residents' annual wine auction.

After inquiring in "Admissions" if there were anyone on the staff named Groon or Janss, then making the rounds of the various treatment centers, taking time to show Ellsie's picture, Hallie took off. No one recognized the photo or the names.

Her luck took a leap, however, at the equally up-to-the-minute St. Helena Hospital, a short distance away. The head supervisor in Home Care Services said the picture resembled Ellsie Janss, one of their trained staff members who provided personal aid to patients.

Monday was Ellsie's day off, and no, the Supervisor couldn't give out her address, but pressed for time, she rattled off a phone number.

After paying ten dollars to a "free" reverse phone lookup service online, Hallie had what she was searching for: an address.

— Chapter 65 —

WITH THE HELP OF HER MAP, her GPS, and her instincts, Hallie found South Crane Road in the picturesque town of St. Helena. Some of the house numbers were blocked by trees or overgrown flora. Fortunately, the GPS led Hallie to her destination.

Parking was easy on the quiet street, and the small, white, wine country cottage with the triangular roof and shuttered windows, seemed almost inviting. On closer look, the front lawn needed attention, and the facade begged for paint, but the house still held its charm.

Taking a few moments to practice her lines, Hallie sat in the car, gathering her thoughts. The approach was crucial. An ill-chosen word or gesture, and she'd be out the door – that is, assuming she'd first gotten in the door.

Finally, her speech rehearsed, she headed for the entrance. One hand carried her purse with a running tape recorder. The other hand held an official-looking "Deputy Police" card Lieutenant Kaiser had once given her. She pressed the bell.

"Who's there?" called a voice.

"I'm Hallie Marsh, an investigator with the San Francisco Police Department," she answered, in her best official tone. "I'll show you my I.D. You're not in trouble and I'm not selling anything."

"What do you want?"

"To talk to you. There's something you should know about the Billings case."

A long silence followed. Hallie rang the bell again.

"I'm not leaving until we talk, Ms. Janss. I have news you need to hear."

More silence, then finally, footsteps sounded, and a frightened head poked around the door. "Show your I.D."

Hallie flashed her card and a smile. "Nice to meet you. I'm Hallie."

Ellsie Janss stared coolly. Then she opened the door. "I suppose you want to come in."

"I won't take much of your time."

Following her reluctant host, whose slippers flip-flopped as she walked, Hallie found herself in a pleasant sitting room. A beige tufted sofa and matching armchair surrounded a glass-topped coffee table. Flowery paper covered the walls, which held a variety of mediocre paintings.

Yet everything seemed neat and well cared for – a contrast to the weed-filled lawn and peeling paint outside. Did she want people to think she was poorer than she was?

Ellsie looked to be in her late fifties, full-figured, with dyed yellow hair that echoed the sunflowers on her house-dress. Red cheeks and freckles did little to enhance her plain features.

"You can sit down," she snapped, "but make it quick. What's this about, anyway?"

"Some new developments in the Billings case. It's being reopened. I thought you'd want to know."

"Why should I care? What new developments?"

"I can't tell you yet. But I'm hoping to ask you some questions and get a few answers so the police won't have to bother you."

"How did you find me?"

"Doesn't matter. If I can find you, Ellsie, anyone can find you."

She frowned. "After all that publicity, I wanted to change my name. People still think I know more than I do. But I couldn't afford to lose my references, change my Social Security, drivers' license, everything – so I settled for just taking back my maiden name. Now what do you want to know?"

"Confirm some facts, please. Mr. and Mrs. Billings had an argument. You were in your room watching television and didn't hear a thing. Mr. Billings' story is that he left the house, went to a bar, came home and discovered that you had found his wife's body and called the police, correct?"

"That's what I told the cops."

"Was your boyfriend with you?"

"No, he came over later to make sure I was okay. He needed an alibi, because Mrs. Billings hated him and she'd warned him not to come around to see me. He blabbed to someone about it, the cops heard about it and figured he had a motive."

"Do you still see him?"

She shook her head. "He died in a motorcycle crash two years ago. He thought he was too good to wear a helmet. And I had a firm alibi. I told the cops exactly what I was watching at the time Mrs. Billings took a spill."

"You think she fell? You think her death was an accident?"

"Had to be. I was with them for four years. They argued, like everyone else, but they were a devoted couple. And why would I want to harm them? I lost the best-paying job I ever had, a job my friends would kill for. Uh-oh, bad choice of words." She seemed to be relaxing, and starting to enjoy the attention.

"Well, I do appreciate your taking a few minutes to talk to me. Incidentally, I can't help admiring those silver candelabra on your mantel."

"Aren't they gorgeous?" Ellsie beamed. "They were a gift from Countess de Baubery when I worked for her. I was polishing them one day, and I told the Countess how beautifiul they were. I guess she took pity on me because she said, 'Oh, Émile gave me some I like better. Would you like to have those?' I couldn't believe what she was saying! I cried and cried, and I thanked her and hugged her. She's the most generous woman."

Ellsie dabbed at an imaginary tear. "What else do you want to know?"

Time for the key question.

Hallie took a long breath. "Suppose I told you there's a possibility Mr. Billings wasn't where he said he was at the time of his wife's death? There's new evidence that might prove him guilty of her murder."

Ellsie stared in surprise. "That's hogwash. I'd just mopped the floor. It was still wet. Mrs. Billings slipped in her fancy shoes and hit the damn statue. But…" Long pause. "Come to think of it, they did have nasty arguments. And I'd sometimes hear Mr. B. on the phone. He had a mean temper. He could sound violent, almost out of control. Sometimes he scared me. Want a drink?"

"No, thanks. I have to be getting back." Hallie stood and offered her hand. "I appreciate your time and your help, Ms. Janss, and I hope the police won't have to bother you."

"Me, too." Seemingly relieved, Ellsie shook hands and led the way to the door. "Nice to meet you, Miss Hallie, but those memories are real painful. I hope I won't see you again."

"I understand." Hallie smiled and let herself out.

— Chapter 66 —

THINKING BACK as she walked to her car, Hallie felt that the meeting, brief as it was, had been worth the effort. Ellsie had taken the bait, jumping on the possibility that new evidence might prove her employer guilty of killing his wife, thus clearing herself as a suspect.

Her statement that Benedict Billings sounded violent was surprising, and not relevant since she had never seen him that way. Yet her observation, if true, was worth noting.

An elderly neighbor, hosing her lawn in the afternoon sun, looked up as Hallie passed by.

"How lucky you are to live here," Hallie called. "It's such a quiet, lovely area."

"We're very fortunate. I saw you come out of Ellsie's house." The woman turned off the faucet, dropped the hose and walked over. She seemed anxious to chat. "We don't see much of her these days. Is she all right?"

"She seems fine. I'm Hallie Marsh from San Francisco. I just came by to bring her news of a mutual friend."

"Nice to meet you. I'm Dorothy. Ellsie's told me and John – that's my husband – all about her life in the big city. This is quite a change for her."

"I don't know her too well." Hallie wasn't about to volunteer information.

"Must've been terrible for her when her grandfather lost all his money. She had us to dinner and told us the sad story a few weeks ago."

"I don't know her background, Dorothy."

"You don't? Well, her grandparents were quite well-

136

to-do and her family lived very upscale – that is, until Grand-
pa made some foolish investments and lost everything they
had."

"How awful!"

Dorothy lowered her voice. "But you should see what
she inherited. Her dishes – I know china, I used to work at
Gump's years ago. Exquisite place plates – what do they call
them now?"

"Chargers."

"Right. And those hand-painted Limoges dishes must
be worth a fortune."

"I'm sure they were lovely."

"Ever heard of Dirk van Erp?"

"Yes, a famous Dutch metalsmith. Why?"

"Get this: Ellsie has a full set of his handmade silverware!"

"A set?"

"Well, we were six for dinner – us, another neighbor
couple, and a retired doctor down the block. We all ate with
the same beautiful flatware. I know it's genuine because one
piece – I think the spoon – was engraved on the back with
van Erp's windmill signature. Even if Ellsie only has six,
they're irreplaceable – and practically priceless. She said she
gets a bit short of money, sometimes, but she'll never sell her
china or silver."

Hallie's mind raced ahead. "Does she own her
house?"

"With a mortgage, I think. The outside needs paint-
ing and I've offered to clean up the lawn for her, but she says
she'll hire a gardener as soon as she can afford it. The other

neighbors don't like it a bit – they say it's an eyesore. I think that's why she had us to dinner – to placate us."

The nosey neighbors apparently knew nothing of the Billings case, and unless they Googled Ellsie Groon instead of Ellsie Janss, they'd continue to be ignorant of her involvement.

Hallie had driven a long way in hopes of getting evidence that Benedict Billings had murdered his wife. Now, however, new facts were making her wonder. While Billings was still her main suspect, Ellsie Groon Janss might also have some questions to answer.

— Chapter 67 —

DETECTIVE TB was firm with Hallie. He wanted no part of her "meddling" in the Billings' case. Lieutenant Helen Kaiser agreed, insisting they had too many current murders to solve to dredge up an old one.

Besides, no one had been convicted in the Billings case, no innocent person was serving time, no one could bring back the dead. If Hallie had some real evidence besides an old picture, they'd take another look.

Determined to find "real evidence," Hallie knew she had to do what she'd hoped the police would do – confront Benedict Billings as a suspect.

Summoning her courage, she called his law offices, dropped her mother's name, and said she'd met the attorney briefly at the Countess de Baubery's Christmas party. Close enough.

Claiming that she had a personal matter to discuss

with him, she refused to reveal what it was. Yet she would be happy to pay for Mr. Billings' time, and after a slew of questions and callbacks, the attorney would see her in two weeks, on Tuesday, March twelfth.

— Chapter 68 —

THE DAY CAME. Photo in hand, questions memorized, Hallie wore a "serious" black suit – with a skirt – and arrived promptly for her 10 o'clock appointment. The receptionist showed her to the lawyer's office.

Dressed casually in wrinkled khakis and a green Polo sport shirt, Benedict Billings stepped around his desk to meet his guest.

He was tall and slightly stooped, Hallie noticed. As his recent online picture showed, the dark wavy hair photographed sixteen years prior, was now gray, matching a neat goatee. No longer was his brow furrowed, his eyes staring anxiously. Although barely recognizable, he appeared relaxed and confident in person.

"I knew your late father – worked on the Museum Board with him. Lovely man," were Billings' first words as he ushered Hallie inside. "Now what's this mysterious problem you couldn't tell my aide about?"

He pulled out a chair and Hallie started to sit. Then suddenly, she stiffened in surprise. "That looks like a Ferrari-red armchair. Would that be a Pininfarina? We studied the world's most expensive chair in my art class."

"You have quite an eye, young lady. It's a cheap copy, of course. I try not to have million dollar furniture lying around. Would you like to try it?"

"No thanks, I'll sit here. I can tell you don't like to waste time, Mr. Billings. Neither do I."

She handed him her Deputy Police Card. "I'm not a policeperson but I do investigative work with the homicide department. Lieutenant Helen Kaiser brought a detail in this photo to my attention. Please look closely."

"Nice shot of your parents," he said, glancing and returning it.

"It was taken on December twenty-third, 1997."

"The day Nina died?"

She handed back the picture. "Please look closer. This was taken at about the same time that your wife was killed. Check the spectators."

Sudden recognition made him blanch, as he stared in shock. "That's me, all right, Ms. Marsh. Oh, to be young and crazy." He reached for a button on a small black box. "I'm no longer recording our interview. That picture proves I was nowhere near my house when Nina died. You say the police saw it? What did they say?"

"That maybe you lied in your alibi. That the picture shows you weren't in the bar all night. That I should look for real evidence."

"Of what, for God's sake? Who the hell asked you to nosey around?" His anger was growing. "Are you going to dredge up this whole horrible tragedy because of one dumb picture? Nina took a spill on a marble floor. No one killed her; it was a horrible accident. We're done here. Now get out of my office and don't come back!"

Hallie rose. "As you wish. But when you see this

picture online, don't sue me. Sue the police."

"Hold on!" he ordered. "Where'd you get the damn picture?"

Hallie turned to face him. "You're quite hostile, Mr. Billings. I hoped you could give me a simple explanation and we could leave the matter alone. There's obviously more to this case than we know. I'm sure the police will want to re-open it."

"Wait!" He scratched his head. "I apologize. Maybe you can understand, Ms. Marsh –"

"Hallie."

"All right, Hallie. Please – come back. There's no excuse for my outburst, except that I've tried to put Nina's death behind me. She was the love of my life and not a day passes that I don't miss her sweet self. But I've a new wife and a new life now and I don't want this dark cloud hanging over us. Most of all, I don't want to have to relive that tragic night. I didn't kill Nina, and if someone did, it's too late to care. The explanation of that picture goes much, much deeper. If it were to appear online, it would ruin several lives, not just my own."

"Oh, dear, I had no idea." Hallie's response was genuine. "I thought perhaps you'd strolled over from the bar and wondered what all the people were looking at, so you joined the crowd."

"I did stroll over from the bar and I did join the crowd. That part is true. The rest is very, very private and no crime was involved, save perhaps the crime of passion. May we leave it there?"

"I can't lie to the police, Mr. Billings."

"The name's Ben." He paused a moment, then said, with some resentment, "All right. You're obviously an honorable woman from a fine family. I'm going to have to trust you, Hallie. May I take you to lunch? And may I ask that you not say anything to anybody until you've heard my story?"

Her eyes widened. "Yes. I promise."

"I'm in court tomorrow. Thursday? Friday?"

"Thursday."

"Thursday it is. Meet me at noon in the Oak Room at the St. Francis. I'll get a quiet table."

"I'll be there." She watched him wipe his forehead. "And don't worry. I'll keep my word."

— Chapter 69 —

SOFT LIGHTING, rose-colored leather chairs that complemented the wood-paneled walls, white-coated servers and well-dressed customers lent the Oak Room a quiet elegance.

Benedict Billings was waiting in a back booth when Hallie entered the restaurant. She spotted him immediately, and slid in beside him.

"You're as prompt as I am," she said, smiling. "My husband says it's one of my faults."

"It's a blessing." His tone was low and serious. "I've been sitting here for half an hour wondering if I'm doing the right thing. I wasn't exaggerating when I said that what I'm about to tell you could ruin many lives if it became known."

"That's a decision only you can make, Mr. Bill – er, Ben."

"I know. And I very much want my wife's death solved. Some of our former friends won't even talk to me. They think I killed her. Do you think I killed her?"

"I don't know. Did you?"

"No, I loved her. I never laid a hand on her. You said the police know about the picture?"

"Lieutenant Helen Kaiser and Detective Baer saw it."

"Then I must confide in you, Hallie. I assume you have influence with them. If what I'm going to say makes sense, I hope you'll do the right thing."

"If I believe what you say, and if I share your strong feelings, I assure you I'll act honorably."

"Good enough." He handed her a menu. "I recommend the onion soup, and if you like sea scallops –"

"Both sound wonderful."

The waiter took their orders and disappeared.

"Times like these I really miss a cigarette." Billings gave a deep sigh. "Where to begin? At the beginning, I guess. The year was 1979. I was thirty years old. A couple of close friends invited us to a dinner party. Nina was going off to visit her mother in Newport Beach, and she asked me to go to the party and represent her, which I did. My dinner partner at the table was a beautiful young woman named Laura, whose husband was also out of town."

"I get the picture," said Hallie.

"I hadn't met Laura before. But as we chatted, I began to feel a strong attraction. I'd never cheated on Nina, and never intended to. Yet I admit I felt a tinge of excitement when she asked if I'd give her a ride home."

"Which you did."

143

"Which I did. I made the mistake of driving out to the beach and parking by the water. I won't mince words. We started kissing, next thing I remember, we were in the back seat making out like two horny teenagers. Then I took Laura home and that was that. I think I need a drink. Some wine?"

"No thanks. I know this is hard for you. Please…take a breather."

— Chapter 70 —

BILLINGS CRADLED his wine glass as the waiter set down their soups. He took several long sips, then picked up his story. "There were no follow-up phone calls, no regrets, no secret trysts, nothing. Neither of us wanted an affair. It was just something that happened. Our spouses never knew, and I forgot about it."

"But?"

"Ah yes, 'But.' Fast-forward fifteen years. Nina and I go to a wedding at the Burlingame Club. After the ceremony, at the reception, I notice a lovely woman staring at us. She looks familiar but I don't remember her at all. In my mind, you see, that incident never happened." He stopped to taste his soup. "Ah, excellent."

The wine seemed to be relaxing him.

"Delicious," agreed Hallie. "I think I can guess who the woman was."

"Of all things, Nina knew her from the Symphony Board and introduced us. Laura was very proper and cool, and we shook hands. The minute I looked into her eyes, though, it all came back…so clearly. I thought I was going to faint."

"You didn't, I hope."

"Thank the Lord, no. Then Laura's husband came up and she introduced him, along with their attractive fifteen-year old daughter, Laurina. I took one look at the girl and I knew in two seconds. She was a foot taller than her father, and the image of her blonde mother, but she had my dark curly hair and brown eyes – even my mouth."

"Your daughter."

"Yes, my daughter! I figured out the timing and she had to be. The panicked look on Laura's face made me realize I had to hold myself together. My heart was about to jump out of my body as I shook my daughter's hand and mumbled a few words. I could hardly keep from embracing her. I have this picture engraved on my brain – of Laura's husband bragging about his daughter's grades, calling her 'Daddy's girl,' and looking at her so lovingly…are you beginning to understand?"

"If I understand so far, you've never told this to anyone. Only two people – you and Laura – know the truth about Laurina."

"And now three people know. And I pray it stops there. But you're wondering about the connection to the tragedy."

"Not really," said Hallie. "If my guess is right, you somehow found out that Laurina was making her debut at the Cotillion that night. You'd had an argument with Nina, you went to your favorite bar near your office, you were drinking heavily, and suddenly you remembered Laurina.

You decided to walk a block or so to see if you could catch a glimpse of her entering the Palace Hotel."

"Good guess. I'd seen a picture of the debs in the morning *Chronicle*, and just as you said, I knew she was 'coming out' that night. I was ten sheets to the wind and completely irrational, or I would've realized that the debutantes had to be there hours earlier. But I poked into the crowd to watch the guests file in, and that's when someone – God knows who –snapped that damn picture."

"That night – what did you do next?"

"I was going to go home, then I remembered that I'd left my hat in the bar, so I went back. When I got there, it was dark and noisy and some guy had passed out with his head on my table, and my hat resting on his head. I realized that the bartender thought the guy was me, and had set down another drink and my bill. I woke the guy up, shooed him away, put on my hat, paid the bartender and went home."

"When you got there, you found the police…and Nina's body?"

"The worst night of my life!" He finished his wine. "I had no idea I'd need an alibi for anything, but the bartender later swore under oath that I was in the bar the whole evening. He was sure I was! And nobody could prove otherwise until you spotted me in that picture. Now, Hallie, I swear every word I'm telling you is the absolute truth. I adored Nina. I've never gotten over losing her. Tell me please – what are you going to do?"

— Chapter 71 —

THIS TIME, it was Hallie who sighed. After several minutes, she spoke slowly. "I share your concern, Ben. The person we must think about is Laurina. And I agree – the truth would shatter her as well as her doting parents and all their friends and relatives, not to mention what it would do to your life. The only possible reason to tell her the truth would be if you had some terrible disease in your genes that she could prepare for. Do you?"

He smiled. "I'm healthy as an ox, assuming oxen are healthy."

"Do you have children of your own?"

"No. Nina had a bad skiing accident when she was nineteen. She couldn't get pregnant. I knew that when I married her, but I was so in love, it didn't matter."

"Did you ever think about adopting?"

"We planned to adopt. We had a special room in the house for 'Baby B'. But we kept putting it off…when we get back from Europe, when we finish retrofitting the house, after Nina's mother's surgery…there was always something."

"How old was Nina –"

"Nina was only forty-four when she died. She was so beautiful. Slim, like you, and a few inches shorter. We were still planning to adopt." He paused as the waiter refilled his wine glass. "Look, Hallie. If you could manage to forget what I just told you, no harm will be done and I'll be eternally in your debt. Should you ever need legal services, you'll have them free for life."

"That's very generous of you, but not necessary."

How painful it must be, she thought, to have no children of your own, and a daughter you can never know or acknowledge. Her tone softened. "I realize the need to keep your secret, and I'll do everything I can to do so, but I won't lie if I'm asked a direct question."

"Fair enough."

"I confess when I first identified you in the picture, and read about the murder, I was sure you were guilty. Now I'm not so sure. It's a weird coincidence, because I'm working on another case where the wife died in strange circumstances. Her husband also thinks it was an accident."

"You mean Andi Douvier? I was following that, but haven't seen much lately. Is anything happening?"

"The police are still investigating."

"Good." The waiter set down two plates of sea scallops. "Smells great, doesn't it? You know, Hallie, I tried Googling you the other day, and you keep such a low profile, I couldn't find out anything. Would you be willing to tell me a bit about yourself? You mentioned your husband. Who's the lucky man?"

— Chapter 72 —

To Hallie's delight, the "lucky man" had just returned from a week in New York, and was pleased to be back, dining at home. Hallie had made herself a tuna salad, Cas was enjoying Stauffer's Baked Chicken Breast, and he could see that her mind was churning.

"Was it today you had lunch with that lawyer who killed his wife?" he asked.

"Yes, but I'm not sure he killed her."

"Then what are you thinking about? Your mind's a thousand miles away."

"I'm sorry, darling." She smiled and turned to him. "How was your trip?"

"Uneventful. Tell me about the lawyer. What's his name? Is he handsome?"

"Billings. Benedict Billings. He's not my type. And too old. He's got a gray beard. But I think he's a good man. Told me a secret that could ruin a lot of lives if known. I can't tell you what it is."

"That's okay, honey. I've some secrets, too." He quickly added, "but it works better if I don't know you have a secret. If I know, I get nervous. Are you having an affair?"

She laughed and kissed him. "Just with you, darling. I couldn't have one, even if I wanted to. You read me like a book."

"A mystery book," he said, pretending to frown. "I think I'd better stay in town for a while."

— Chapter 73 —

A CALL to Detective TB the next morning, Friday, proved frustrating to Hallie. TB's partner, Lenny, answered the phone, explaining that they were still deeply involved in the Douvier case, still following new leads. He said they'd received the lab reports about the shoes, and none of the saliva, blood, or hair samples matched Andi's DNA. He added that since the visitors to the wine room weren't considered murder suspects, he could send her their forty-two names, as she'd requested.

Next came a call from Benedict Billings' aide, offering Hallie two tickets to the Symphony that Saturday night. She regretted, saying they were busy. Then she asked if Mr. Billings would phone her when he had a minute.

The minute came quickly. "Got your message, Hallie," he said. "Problems?"

"Everything's fine," she assured him. "I just forgot to tell you that I went to see Ellsie Groon. She goes by Ellsie Janss now."

"Good Lord, where'd you see Ellsie?"

"In St. Helena. She works at a hospital there. She had kind words to say about you."

"She's a good woman. How's she doing?"

"Fine, it seems. Keeping a low profile. Did you know she came from a wealthy family?"

"Ellsie?" He laughed. "No way! We checked her up, down and sideways before we hired her. We know her parents and grandparents were fishermen – good, honest working folks, but wealthy? No. Where'd you get that idea?"

"One of her neighbors told me she'd had dinner at Ellsie's house and heard all about her rich grandparents. She said Ellsie had beautiful china and silver she'd inherited from them. You think she was just trying to impress her neighbor?"

"It's possible. Or maybe she was pretending her stuff was better than it was."

"Maybe." Hallie took a few seconds to digest the information. "Have you heard of Dirk van Erp?"

"Of course. Nina had a set of silverware Dirk van Erp made for her mother. She was very proud of it."

Hallie's ears perked. "What happened to it?"

"It's in storage in our basement. Pamala, my wife, didn't want it, she had her own silver. She took what she wanted of Nina's things, including her jewelry, and we had Ellsie pack up the rest when we moved. Ellsie's quite strong, you know. She amazed us by lifting and carrying those heavy boxes –" He stopped himself. "You don't think…?"

"I don't know. Do you remember how much silver you had?"

"In fact I do. Nina loved to give small dinner parties. We never had extra guests, because we only had silver service for twelve. We used to joke about it – what we'd do if the President was a last minute guest."

"Seriously, Ben, did you ever check the silver and dishes Ellsie packed?"

"You mean count them? No, Nina and I had total trust in Ellsie. And I'm – you understand – I get pretty emotional when I go through Nina's things. Pamala kept a lot of Nina's art objects, but she's always at me to go through the basement boxes and sell the rest of the stuff at auction. I keep putting it off."

"If I were you," Hallie said quietly. "I wouldn't put it off any longer."

— Chapter 74 —

LATE MONDAY MORNING, Hallie emailed Billings to ask if

he'd had time to search his basement over the weekend. Apparently he hadn't. His answer didn't come back till Thursday. She read it anxiously:

"Dear Hallie, I'm sorry to report that your instincts were correct. Our silver service is down to six, as are Nina's Limoges dishes. A box of her favorite lace placemats is half-empty. Also, a Miró etching we picked up in Paris and a Picasso sculpture we bought in Spain are missing. I didn't pay much attention to the other art works, but I remember those two because we bought them on our honeymoon. I made the mistake of telling that to Pamala and she had Ellsie pack them away with the other things."

The message continued: *"I find it hard to believe that Ellsie would steal, and my first thought was to blame the boyfriend, but he would have sold the goods, and Ellsie seems to be using them herself — unless she's just dropping names and pretending.*

"My instinct is to say, 'The hell with it — I don't have time to bother.' But Nina would be furious, so I'll pursue it — with your help, I hope. We don't have enough evidence for a search warrant, do we? Is there any way you can get invited to Ellsie's house for dinner?"

Possible scenarios raced through Hallie's brain, and just as quickly, she rejected them. Ellsie was too smart and too suspicious to fall for some ruse. It would tip her off, and if she did have damaging evidence, she'd find a way to hide or dispose of it.

The answer, Hallie decided, was to enter Ellsie's house legally, with a search warrant. But how in the world would she get one?

— Chapter 75 —

PEOPLE FIND IT HARDER to say no to you in person, Hallie reflected, looking back on her twelve years in Public Relations. When she wanted to insert a name in the media, she would often pay a visit to the newspaper office, radio or TV station. If the person she hoped to see was unavailable, she would leave a handwritten letter and a press kit, so her request would at least be noticed. And about one time out of three, her visits paid off.

So it was that on a Friday morning, the day after receiving Billings' message, she drove down to the police station in the Hall of Justice. The officer at the entrance recognized her and waved her inside, assuming she had an appointment.

Bypassing the main area where Detective TB had his desk, she headed for Lieutenant Kaiser's office, knocked, and was told to enter.

Helen Kaiser was watching a video and motioned Hallie to take a chair. After several minutes, Helen turned off her speakers, stood, and offered her hand. "To what murder do I owe this pleasure?" she asked.

"The Billings case. May I take five minutes?"

"Is this something TB could help you with?"

"No, because I need you to listen to what I've found out so you'll let me peek at the file."

With a sigh, Helen sank into her chair. "Okay – talk fast."

Hallie quickly summarized the difficulties she had finding Ellsie, and why she thought Billings' explanation of the picture plausible – i.e. that he was drunk, saw a group of people and just wandered over. There was no need to reveal his secret.

In essence, Hallie was no longer sure that he was guilty of murder, and had good reason to suspect that Ellsie had stolen the missing silver, dishes, placemats and art. Was she also capable of murder?

The problem, Hallie explained, was that she needed evidence to convince a judge that a search warrant was justified. If the items turned up at Ellsie's house, and she believed they would, the former maid would at least be guilty of larceny.

Helen listened carefully to Hallie's story, then surprised her by reaching into a stack of folders and pulling one out. "Have Billings make a police report with pictures, if possible, of the remaining silver and china," she said. "It will go into our national database of stolen items."

"Will do."

"You've done your homework, Hallie. Here's the Billings case. Go over to the table, make copies of what you want, go home, and don't come back until you're sure you have a viable suspect. Take whatever new clues you find to homicide – that is, if you find anything we've missed. I'll alert TB. I shouldn't even be discussing this with you. Got it?"

"Got it." Hallie grabbed the file before the Lieutenant could change her mind. "Thanks," she said, with a wave.

— Chapter 76 —

THAT EVENING, Cas came home shortly after five to find his wife standing in a sea of papers. Documents, photos,

154

scribbled notes and scraps of paper were strewn across her desk and spread out on the floor.

He leaned over and kissed her cheek. "What happened to that super-neat woman I married? Your office looks like mine."

"I know. Your ex-girlfriend let me make copies of the Billings file."

"Helen Kaiser? How is the old gal?"

"Great, but I'm going crazy. I really need you, sweetheart. Will you help me?"

"Uh – sure. *After* dinner."

By 10 o'clock that night, Hallie was feeling tired and frustrated. Together, she and Cas had read and discussed almost every aspect of the unsolved mystery, SFPD Case 397-82109B.

Unable to reach firm conclusions, Cas leaned toward Benedict Billings as the culprit, especially since he had started openly dating Pamala only six weeks after Nina's death.

Hallie was working on her own theories, that Ellsie and her boyfriend had engineered the murder, that a would-be burglar, delivery person or "friend" had done the deed, or that it was, in fact, an accident.

Thoroughly exhausted, they were about to quit when Cas spotted a close-up photo of the blouse Nina was wearing when she died. Although Ellsie's prints were clearly outlined in several places, the police had accepted her explanation that she'd ironed the garment "just before Mrs. Billings put it on," and then helped her get into it.

Cas squinted, reached for a magnifier and peered

closely. "I'm reading the label," he said. "Why would Ellsie iron a blouse that says 'Permanent Press'?"

"Nice try, honey, but permanent press clothes often need touching up, especially if the wearer's fussy."

He kept squinting. "All these fingerprints could be from ironing. But look at this pair of palm prints – they're exactly the same – the amount of pressure, the way they're aligned. They had to be made at the same time, both hands at once."

Hallie's face lit up. "Ellsie couldn't have been ironing at the time."

"And those palm prints couldn't have been made when Ellsie was helping Nina Billings put it on. Those prints had to be made when Nina was wearing the blouse."

"Yes." Hallie was pensive for a few seconds. "I remember Ben Billings telling me how beautiful Nina was. He said she was shorter than I, but she was wearing three-inch heels. Ellsie would've been about six inches shorter than Nina. If I stand on something, and you press your hands against my T-shirt, we'll know where Ellsie was touching Nina."

"Not very scientific."

"Humor me." She reached under her desk for a footrest, slipped off her sweater, and stood on the stool. "Now come closer and place your hands on my upper chest – about seven inches apart."

Nodding, Cas opened his hands and placed them on her T-shirt. "My fingers are touching your shoulder bones."

"Good. Now push me – hard!"

Following orders, he gave her a shove. With a cry, she

tumbled backwards, falling off the stool, but catching her balance and landing on her feet.

"Thanks, darling," she said, hugging him. "I think we can go to sleep now."

PART 12

— Chapter 77 —

ON A FOGGY MONDAY, ten days later, Hallie kept her 2 p.m. appointment with Detective TB. Complaining of being "bogged down," he'd put her off till the first day he had "just five minutes" to see her.

Sitting opposite his desk, controlling her frustration at his lack of interest in the case, she told him about calling on Ellsie Janss, and how she'd asked Benedict Billings about the silver.

Then she handed him a copy of Billings' police report, pictures he'd taken of the remaining dishes, silverware, and placemats, and a short summary of why he agreed with Hallie that the missing items were likely to be found in Ellsie's house.

Skeptical as always, TB tried to send Hallie to the Property Crimes Division, but she insisted that new evidence indicated that Ellsie had lied in her testimony. The fact that the palm prints on Nina's blouse showed that Ellsie had "put hands" on her employer, were another probable cause for a search warrant," she told him.

Reluctantly, TB agreed to present the evidence to a judge.

That evening, after Hallie and Cas celebrated Danny's first birthday, she took a call from TB's partner Lenny.

"Sorry, your request for a search warrant was denied," he told her. "The Judge said a neighbor's gossip about silver and dishes is not probable cause, it's hearsay. And even if you'd seen the objects in Ellsie's house, it would still only be circumstantial evidence."

"And the palm prints on Nina Billings' blouse?"

"I'm not sure TB even mentioned them. They weren't relevant to the theft."

"What?" Hallie exclaimed. "They practically *prove* Ellsie struck her employer! Don't you want to catch a possible murderer?"

"I'll talk to TB," he said calmly. "Right now, we're drowning in work."

— Chapter 78 —

THE NEXT MORNING, Hallie was still simmering as she pondered what to do. Checking her email, she saw a message from Detective TB. It was a copy of a page he had added to the Billings file. She read:

"On Monday, April 1, 2013, private citizen/amateur crime-solver Hallie Marsh called on Detective Theodore Baer. On her own time, Ms. Marsh has been attempting to investigate the 1997 unsolved death of Nina Billings, SFPD Case 397-82109B. Three suspects were questioned.

"With the help of Detective Lenny Brisco, Detective Baer agreed to check evidence that Ms. Marsh claims was previously overlooked. Two crash test dummies were configured to approximate the height and weight of the victim, Nina Billings, and her housemaid, suspect Ellsie Janss, formerly Ellsie Groon.

"The forensic lab re-enacted a scene where the placement of Elsie Janss's palm prints on the victim's blouse confirmed that she had 'put hands' on her employer. Still unconfirmed is whether

the suspect used excessive force, causing the vic to fall back and hit her head against a bronze statue, resulting in the fatal subdural hematoma.

"One must seriously question Ms. Janss's claim that she went to her room after cleaning the kitchen, and did not see her employer again until she found her body and called the police.

"At the same time, new evidence indicates that Mr. Billings' alibi for the time of his wife's death is no longer valid. The third suspect in the case is deceased.

"Medical Examiner Dr. Thomas Toy estimates TOD between 9:20 and 9:30 p.m. The police received a call at 9:41 p.m., and arrived at the possible crime scene at 9:52. The body was warm.

"Still to be determined is whether additional evidence is needed, or whether the two remaining suspects can be brought in for questioning.

"Attached is a copy of a recent Police Report in which the victim's husband, Benedict Billings, reports the discovery of missing valuables, and has strong reason to suspect Ms. Janss.

"The investigation continues."

— Chapter 79 —

THAT EVENING, a delighted Hallie read Cas the email from TB. They were sitting on the sofa in their living room, watching Danny play with his toys and waddle around the room. All small and breakable objects had been moved to a high bookshelf.

"Is that memo good news?" asked Cas.

"Fabulous!" Hallie cuddled up to him. "TB's finally

taking an interest in the case, but how can I find additional evidence? I've been thinking all day, and every brilliant scheme I dream up would be thrown out of court."

"For being obtained illegally?"

"Yes. They always find loopholes. I don't even know what's legal and what isn't anymore. Why can't they just bring Ellsie in for questioning?"

"Handprints on a blouse aren't conclusive evidence of murder."

"She may not realize that."

"But the police do. And from what you've told me, they still aren't sure that it was a murder. I doubt they'd bring someone in for questioning about petty larceny. It's only a misdemeanor in California. If the stolen items are worth more than $400, then it's grand larceny and it's a felony."

"Are you serious? They're worth much more than that! The problem is we don't have a motive – a reason why Ellsie would push her employer so hard that she cracks her skull against a statue. What were she and Nina talking about? Supposedly, Ellsie loved her employer, and loved her job even more."

"Beats me, honey. And in case you haven't noticed, Danny's climbed up on your white chair and he's about to knock over your flowers."

"Whoops!" Hallie dashed across the room and scooped up her son just as he reached for a vase of blossoms. "You are *so* nosey," she whispered, hugging him. "Guess it runs in the family."

— Chapter 80 —

BEFORE HALLIE COULD FINISH her cereal the next morning, a call came from Benedict Billings.

"Got a minute? I have news for you," he said, not waiting for an answer. "I went to see Ellsie last Sunday."

"You did?"

"Yes, I've been meaning to tell you, just too busy. We've a home in Napa – go there almost every weekend. My aide got Ellsie's phone number from the St. Helena hospital where you told me she worked. I called Ellsie, said it was important I talk to her, and she agreed to see me."

"And –?"

"She tried to be pleasant. Wanted to know if the case had been reopened, and I told her it had never been closed. I mentioned that there was new evidence possibly incriminating me."

"What did she say?"

"That some lady who worked with the cops had come to see her, and that she'd insisted I was a fine gentleman and would never have harmed Nina."

"That's a lie, Ben! She first told me that Nina's death was accidental, but she was quick to agree with me that you were a suspect. She also said you have a mean temper, you often sounded violent on the phone, and that she was scared of you."

"She said that?"

"I have her on tape."

"Hmm. I suspected she was two-faced – a mite too perfect to be believable. Yet she had Nina eating out of her hand. Nina was missing some jewelry and a few other things during the four years Ellsie was with us, but Nina was sure it was the boyfriend. She was shocked to learn from the doorman that Ellsie 'entertained' him in the house on weekends, when we were in the country. She was going to scold Ellsie, and forbid the sleazebag to set foot in our house. I don't know if Nina ever got around to telling Ellsie. We talked about it the morning she died."

Hallie groaned. "The sleazebag's dead, so he can't tell us. Did you find out anything about the silver and dishes?"

"You bet. I told her I was getting Nina's possessions ready for auction and noticed that we only had service for six, not twelve. She pretended to be surprised that I didn't know Nina had said she was through entertaining at home, and had given her the silver and dishes as a gift."

"Oh, no!"

"I was furious," he went on, "but I kept my cool and didn't call her a freakin' liar. She mumbled something about Babe de Baubery's having given her some fancy candlesticks, too."

"Yes," Hallie said. "I checked with the Countess and was amazed to learn that Babe *did* give Ellsie a pair of candelabra. Is there any chance Nina really did give Ellsie the missing items?"

"No. I know she stole them."

"Knowing isn't proving, Ben."

He sighed into the phone. "It's true that Nina wasn't keen on hosting dinner parties. She said it was too much work, even with caterers. She'd read somewhere that dinner parties at home were 'out' and people 'in the know' took guests to their private clubs."

"In that frame of mind, might she have given the maid her precious silver?

"No way!"

"I believe you."

"You haven't heard the best. She said she's coming to town to see her brother this weekend, and she actually offered to polish my silver and get it ready for the auction."

Hallie shook her head in disbelief. "That's incredible. Can we get her arrested for chutzpah?"

"Talk to the cops," he said. "I can't get too involved. I'm still a suspect."

— Chapter 81 —

DETECTIVE TB was almost friendly when Hallie sat down opposite his desk that afternoon. The station looked near empty. Except for the ringing of phones, the usual clamor of voices had been replaced by a low volume of chatter and even occasional laughter.

Air Force One would be landing at the San Francisco airport in two-and-a-half hours, TB explained, and much of the police force would be helping control the crowds hoping for a glimpse of the President.

"So – you're here for a reason," he said, wasting no time on niceties. "Which case have you solved for us, Douvier or Billings?"

Hallie forced a smile. She couldn't very well complain about his sarcasm; Lieutenant Kaiser thought he was the best detective on the force.

"Mr. Billings phoned me this morning," she answered. "Said he'd seen Ellsie, the housekeeper, who admitted she had the 'missing' items, but insisted they were a gift from his wife, Nina."

"Is that possible?"

"Not according to Billings."

"And you believed him? Hallie, for God's sake, have you forgotten he's our main suspect? That picture you showed us proved he was not where he said he was at the time Nina died."

"He has an explanation," she said, momentarily caught off guard.

"And pray tell, what is that?"

"Umm – he said he left the bar for five minutes to get some air, poked his head into the crowd at the Palace Hotel, where they were having an event, then went right back to the bar. He was gone such a short time, the bartender, who swore he was in the bar all night, never noticed."

"So what do we have now – the husband's lame excuse and the housemaid's handprints?"

"It's not a lame excuse!" She startled herself by sounding so adamant. "I mean – can't we question Ellsie first?"

"She lives in Napa. That's for the local P.D."

"But the alleged crime took place here. And Ben Billings said she was coming here this weekend to see her brother. I have a hunch my visit and Ben's appearing at her front door might have set off an alarm. I'm pretty sure she'll be staying with her brother. He's quite protective of her."

TB scratched his head. "Do we know where the brother lives?"

"I'll find out, TB," she promised. "I'll get back to you."

— Chapter 82 —

ONCE HOME, Hallie immediately called her confidante, Sara Redington. After filling her in on the case history, she told of her difficulty finding out where Howard Janss lived. Internet sources showed only his work address.

"And I suppose you need an accomplice for whatever devious scheme you've dreamed up?" asked Sara. "Why else would you be calling me at the time you always take Danny for a walk."

"It so happens I do have a plan. What are you and Dale doing this weekend?"

"Joanne and Rick asked us for dinner Saturday night. Unlike somebody whose name I won't mention, Joanne likes to cook. Why?"

"Perfect. They live on Russian Hill and it's impossible to park around there. So it would make sense to hire someone to drive you there and back, right?"

"Wrong. Cabs are cheaper."

"Hush, Sara. A practical woman like you doesn't rely on cabs. You're going to call a firm called 'Drivers 4U,' and say a friend recommended Howard Janss, and is he available Saturday night for – say four hours?"

"And if they say yes?"

"Then you hire Janss for Saturday night. He drives his own car to your house at 7 o'clock or whatever time you want him. Then he parks, and drives you and Dale – in *your*

167

car – to Joanne and Rick's condo. He waits for you and Dale, and drives you home about 11. Then he drives himself home in his own car. Got it?"

"I suppose so, unless he has a late date."

"He won't," said Hallie emphatically. "His sister's visiting. As soon as he leaves your house, I follow him home and voilà! I get his address."

"What if he spots you following him?"

"I'll get Cas to help me. We'll change places along the way so Janss won't see the same car trailing him. Just think: if all goes well, you'll have the satisfaction of having helped solve a murder."

Sara exhaled loudly. "Sometimes I wish you weren't my best friend. Why do you have to keep chasing murderers? Can't you go to a Scrabble Tournament or something? Can't you just sit back and enjoy your beautiful family?"

"You're my soul mate, Sara, I know I can count on you. Oops, thanks for reminding me – I almost forgot Danny's walk!"

— Chapter 83 —

SEVERAL PHONE CHATS LATER, the plan changed. Cas had been called out of town before Hallie could tell him of the weekend's agenda. Knowing he would object to her following a strange man God-knows-where at a late hour, she conveniently forgot to mention it.

That Saturday night, as she sat watching "Law and Order," the phone rang.

"We're leaving Joanne and Rick's place," whispered

Sara. "We'll be home in twenty minutes."

"I'll be there," said Hallie.

In the darkness, parked nearby, Hallie could see the Redingtons' blue BMW pull up to their driveway. Howard Janss got out, opened the door for his passengers, then handed Dale Redington a clipboard. Dale scribbled his name, locked their BMW, and he and Sara went inside.

Janss strolled down the street, presumably to get his own car.

He continued walking another two blocks, as Hallie watched with interest. Then he turned the corner.

What to do? Even though the quiet residential district seemed safe, she was reluctant to follow him on foot. Fortunately, the motor in her Prius was almost silent. Driving to the corner where he'd turned, she saw him continue on to busy California Street. If he hopped on a bus, that would be easy, she thought.

But he didn't. The street veered to the right at 8th Avenue, causing Hallie to lose him. "Damn!" she said aloud.

Moments later, however, she spotted him, still walking along California Street, never looking back, his step now lively. Pausing for a red light at Park Presidio, where signs directed drivers to the Golden Gate Bridge, he checked his watch, then resumed his path.

Hallie kept him constantly in view, slowing down at each intersection, staying a block or two behind, careful to keep out of sight.

Twenty minutes later, still walking briskly, Howard Janss rounded the corner at 21st Avenue. Half-way down the street, he turned into what looked to be a well-kept duplex.

Hallie's heart beat fast. She decided to risk driving slowly by, passing Janss as he climbed a brick stairway, inserted a key and entered the left of two doorways. House numbers were nowhere to be seen, and Hallie dared not stop. But the address of the apartment building next door was clearly visible. Memorizing it, she had all the information she needed.

With a silent "Hallelujah!" she drove to the end of the block and headed home.

— Chapter 84 —

THE NEXT DAY, Sunday, Hallie returned to 21st Avenue, found a parking spot, and took a stroll down the street. The duplex where she'd last seen Howard Janss was pale blue stucco in the daylight, and she recognized the brick staircase. The address over the door was faded, and had skipped her notice the night before, but she could see it now and jotted it down.

Her patience, what there was of it, was almost non-existent Monday morning, as she pondered the best and fastest way to reach TB.

Despite the temptation to phone or text him and request a call back, which he might make in a day or two, or whenever he felt like it, she decided to try the number he'd given her (probably in a weak moment) for emergencies. To her disappointment, the number was disconnected and referred her to 9-1-1.

Reluctantly, she scribbled an email:

"Subject: The Billings Case

"Dear TB, I was able to get the address of Howard Janss (see attached), who's the brother of Ellsie Janss, one of our suspects. Please consider trying again for a search warrant. Ellsie Janss is reportedly staying with Howard this weekend, and I've a strong hunch she might have brought the items she allegedly stole – either to hide in her brother's house or to sell here.

"Forgive my impatience, but it's imperative you act today, while Ellsie still (hopefully) has the goods. Perhaps you could tell the Judge about the palm prints on Nina Billings' blouse, which indicate Ellsie's involvement in a possible homicide. Please call if I can help. Thanks."

Late that afternoon, Detective Lenny Brisco phoned Hallie. "TB wants you to know we got the warrant," he said. "We've finished searching and we're about to leave Howard Janss's house. The specified property was not found."

"That's good news about the warrant, but are you sure you searched everywhere? No silver? No dishes?" she asked.

"Nope."

"You searched Howard's car?"

"Not there, either."

"Did you search Ellsie's car?"

"No. Where is it?"

"Why don't you ask Ellsie. Is she there?"

"Yeah, I'll go ask her."

"And Lenny," she said, "please check under the seats,

171

and the trunk, top to bottom, even if there's lots of stuff in there."

"Okay, Hallie, I'm on it."

— Chapter 85 —
The Next Afternoon

GRATEFUL TO HAVE BEEN INVITED, Hallie stood with Lieutenant Helen Kaiser outside one of the Interrogation Rooms in the police station. Peering through the one-way glass, they could see what was going on inside, and hear the conversation from a speaker.

According to the Lieutenant, Ellsie had told the police who searched her brother's house, that she'd given her dishes and silver to the Salvation Army to "avoid complications." The items, however, were later found buried deep in the trunk of her car. Although the police had no warrant for Ellsie's arrest, discovery of the allegedly stolen goods gave them probable cause to take her in for questioning.

The two women watched intensely as TB took a chair opposite Ellsie Janss. Howard Janss sat beside his sister. Lenny paced back and forth, glaring at the suspect.

"Lenny likes to play 'bad cop-good cop' and create tension," said Helen. "Fear tends to make people talk."

Hallie nodded. "I've read about your psychological manipulation. That look would scare me, too!"

TB began the questioning by making sure Ellsie knew her

Miranda rights and didn't want a public defender.

"Why would I want a lawyer?" she asked. "I didn't do anything wrong."

"No one's saying you did, Miss Janss. But perhaps you'll tell us where you got the dishes and silverware we found in your car?"

"I *told* you. Mrs. Billings said she wasn't going to have any more dinner parties," she answered irritably. "I've always admired her pretty things, so she gave me a few and kept the rest."

"Just like that?" Lenny shot back. "A wealthy employer suddenly gives her housekeeper thousands of dollars –"

"Cool it, Brisco!" TB scolded. "Sorry, Miss Janss. Lenny's a bit short on manners."

"Ellsie's telling the truth," insisted Howard Janss. "Rich folks can be mighty generous if they like you. Look at those nice candlesticks the Baroness gave her."

"Countess," corrected Ellsie.

"They're worth three thousand dollars! My sister had them appraised."

"I understand, sir." TB's voice was respectful and reassuring. "Now, Miss Janss, assuming you were pleased with the generous gift from Mrs. Billings, why did you hide them in your car and say you gave them away?"

"I was scared," she said, with a shrug. "First that pushy blonde came to see me, then Mr. Billings told me that the police were accusing him of murder –"

TB shook his head. "Not true. We believe that Mrs. Billings' death could have been accidental."

173

"I'm sure it was. Mr. B. is a nice man. He wouldn't have hurt his wife on purpose. But…"

"But?"

"I'm afraid he does have a terrible temper – even a violent streak. I wouldn't be surprised if he shoved her against that sculpture in a moment of rage. They said they loved each other but they sure fought a lot."

"So you think Mr. Billings is a possible killer?"

"Who else could it be?"

"We'll take that into consideration. We're checking everyone's alibi – even yours, Miss Janss. Didn't you say in your testimony that your fingerprints on Mrs. B.'s blouse were from ironing the garment?"

"Yeah, she wouldn't wear anything with wrinkles."

"Why did you put your hands on her?"

"What?" Ellsie cocked her head. "You mean when I helped button her blouse in the back?"

TB's voice was soft and non-threatening. "No, our forensic lab found your palm prints on the front of her blouse."

She shifted her weight in the chair. "That doesn't prove anything – I mean, if you're insinuating anything. My prints are probably all over the damn blouse."

"Liar!" yelled Lenny. "You shoved her into the statue."

"Shut up, Brisco!" TB shouted back. "Let the woman talk."

Lenny took the cue. "Can't you see she's playing you? The bitch is insulting our intelligence. Why do you listen to her? She's a liar!"

Ellsie jumped to her feet. "I am not a liar! I will tell you the truth. Nina Billings insulted me and threatened me. I thought she was going to strike me so I pushed her away – in self-defense. She was wearing her dumb shoes with the high heels and she lost her balance and fell back. I tried to grab her, but her head hit that metal statue and it was –" A tear rolled down Ellsie's cheek. "Too late."

"If it was self-defense, it wasn't your fault," said TB soothingly, before she could retract. He slid a tissue box towards her. "Why didn't you tell that to the police?"

"I knew it would look bad for me," she said, sniffing. "A beautiful rich lady gets *accidentally* killed by her house-maid? Mr. Billings and his big powerful law firm would grind me to dust in five minutes. How could a poor working woman like me fight back? I wouldn't have had a chance to tell my side of the story. And if I did, no one would've believed me – like you."

TB looked surprised. "I believe you. Accidents happen. You must have had provocation. What were you discussing?"

"My boyfriend Zack." Ellsie wiped her nose. "Mrs. Billings said some things had been stolen and she was going to have him arrested. Zack hadn't stolen anything, and he would've killed me if he were arrested. He had two felonies for drunk driving accidents that injured people. If he had a third felony, the three strikes law would've sent him to prison for life!"

"That's true, Miss Janss." TB took her arm. "Let's sit down and talk quietly. What you say is true. That law was enacted in 1974 with a mandatory life sentence for three

175

felonies. It's been amended several times since, but in 1997, the law was still in its early stages."

"Then you know I'm telling the truth," she said.

"Yes, that explains your impulsive action. You were scared for Zack and for yourself. There was no malice or forethought. You were frightened and upset. You gave your employer a push. You put your hands on her first, which is a minor criminal act. But it's not murder one by a long shot. Nina Billings' death was an unplanned accident – involuntary manslaughter."

"Yeah," she said, starting to cry, as her brother wrapped her in his arms.

"That's right, detective," he agreed. "Ellsie wouldn't lie to the police. Thanks for understanding."

— Chapter 86 —

THE SMILE on Howard Janss's face faded quickly several minutes later, as Ellsie handed her written confession to TB, and assumed she would be going home. Ignoring her cries and protests, a uniformed officer placed Ellsie's hands behind her back and locked her into handcuffs.

"Why are you arresting her?" demanded her brother.

Still playing his role, Lenny snarled, "Try perjury, grand larceny and manslaughter for starters."

"But I told the truth," Ellsie pleaded, looking to TB.

"Calm down, Miss Janss." The detective's voice was no longer sympathetic. "You'll have your day in court."

"What about my silver and dishes?"

"Right now they're evidence. If your story is confirmed and you're freed of the charges, you'll get them back."

"Get me a lawyer, Howard!" she screamed, as the officer led her away.

Lieutenant Kaiser saw no reason why Hallie couldn't call Ben Billings with the news.

It was almost nine that night when he answered his home phone. Hallie's words left him momentarily speechless. Overwhelmed with emotion, he finally said, "Do you know I've waited almost sixteen years to have my name cleared? – To be able to walk into a room without having people pretend they don't see me, or start whispering to their friends? This is the greatest gift you could give me."

"That's wonderful, Ben. I'm glad I could help the truth come out."

"I assume Ellsie will be tried for larceny as well as manslaughter. Did you find my silver?"

"Yes, the police are holding it for evidence. I didn't think you cared about getting it back."

"I do now," he said. "Someday I want to be able to give it to my daughter."

"But your secret is safe," she protested, lowering her voice. "I'll never tell a soul about Laurina and no one ever has to know."

"I'm eternally grateful, Hallie. I can't thank you enough. But I didn't mean Laurina." He paused a few seconds before announcing: "Pamala's five months along. Isabelle Ann Billings is due in July."

PART 13

"GOOD WORK!" said Cas that evening, as Hallie recounted her story. "Now maybe you'll have time to mend my blue sweater."

"Can't we give it to Goodwill?" she asked. "I know I said I'd sew up that seam, but I really don't do rips and tears. Just buttons."

"You want me to pay my tailor twenty bucks to fix a sweater that cost eighteen?"

"Your call, sweetheart." She was standing by his desk as he attempted to work at his computer. "I just had an idea. You know how they arrange marriages in all those foreign countries? Why don't we betroth Danny to Isabelle Ann Billings?"

"One reason might be that she isn't born yet. What if she has two heads? Now may I please get back to work? I have to finish this parking story."

"I hate workaholics," she grumbled.

Five minutes later, Hallie sat at her own computer. An email from Lieutenant Kaiser thanked her for her persistence, and assured her that her name would not be released to the news sources, as she requested.

Several friends checked in, a Nigerian "banker' informed her that a distant relative had left her $7 million, but she needed to mail him $2500 for bank fees.

Various dates and appointments were confirmed, and one message piqued her curiosity: *Golden Gate Star* publisher

Tulip Rosenkrantz, whom she hadn't seen in months, invited her to lunch "Thursday or Friday, someplace where we won't see anyone we know?"

Hallie answered that she was taking Danny for a checkup Thursday, but, "Friday would be great. Meet me at noon at Mel's Drive-In on Van Ness. Great burgers and shakes!"

— Chapter 88 —

TULIP WAS A FEW MINUTES LATE to the midtown diner, a smile on her wrinkle-free face, eyes bright and gleaming behind her moon-shaped specs. As always, her black turtleneck and slacks were immaculate, outlining her full bosom and slim hips. A red velvet ribbon tied back her hair.

Spotting Hallie at a table for two, she hurried past the crowded booths filled with noisy teenagers, weekend daddies with kids, zaftig women feasting on French Fries and hot fudge sundaes.

"Don't get up," Tulip ordered, taking a seat and bestowing an air kiss. "You look good, pussycat. Been waiting long?"

"No, and *you've* never looked better – or happier. What's going on?"

"First fill me in about Andi Douvier. The police won't tell me anything, and they've been so silent – have they given up?"

"Not at all. Before I got sidetracked with the Billings case, they were this close to getting an answer. We were waiting for some reports and TB – the detective – was supposed to keep in touch. Guess I have to remind him."

"Do you read the *Star?*"

"Are you serious? I devour every juicy word. I know you've been tracking the Douvier case, having your writers interview Andi's friends and former employees, and generally, helping keep the mystery alive. I've a good idea what happened, but the police still need conclusive evidence."

Nodding agreement, Tulip reached into her purse and drew out the front page of the two-day-old *Chronicle*. Its bold headline read:

SIXTEEN-YEAR MYSTERY SOLVED
Benedict Billings Cleared

"I was fascinated by this story," she said, "and a little birdie told me who really solved the case. You're amazing. We were all positive Ben was so smitten with Pamala, he knocked off poor Nina. Congratulations!"

"You say so much in so few words," laughed Hallie. "I admit I did some snooping, but it was the police who got the housekeeper to confess. What does that have to do with whatever's on your mind?"

"Everything! Mostly – what you said, that you did some snooping. Pussycat –" She dropped her voice and leaned in closer, "I need you to snoop for me."

— **Chapter 89** —

"I WON'T MINCE WORDS," Tulip went on, after a pause. "I met a younger man at a party at Babe de Baubery's. He's French, divorced, lives in Paris, and is here on a visit. We've been going out. He knows I'm sixty-three, but – well, he says he's *amoureux de moi.* As you can see, I've started taking French lessons."

The alarm sirens in Hallie's head were almost audible. "How much younger?"

"He says he's fifty-five."

"You don't believe him?"

"I do believe him. It's just that he's so generous and *charmant.* He seems too good to be true, and I can't find out much about him. I've Googled him, and he gets mentions in the social pages, but I couldn't find anything about his company. I wrote a friend in France and she couldn't get any info, either. Maybe he just likes to keep a low profile."

Hallie refrained from rolling her eyes. Her tough-minded, sophisticated, slightly jaded publisher friend was acting like a lovesick adolescent.

"To be honest, Tulip, my first instinct is skepticism. Forgive cliché, but if it sounds too good to be true, it isn't. What's his name and what's his business?"

"Pierre Moulet. That's also the name of his company. He says it's a *Fondation de famille* that buys art and donates it to museums. He seems to have *beaucoup d'argent.* He's not extravagant, though. He doesn't throw it around."

The clatter of dishes drowned a sigh. "Look, Tulip, why don't you go online and read about some con artists from the past? If nothing rings your chimes and you're still interested in this French guy, hire a company that does background checks. I'm strictly amateur."

"Oh, I couldn't do that, sugarplum. Pierre's very proud. If he ever found out I was checking up on him, he'd never forgive me."

Unable to think of a quick answer, Hallie grabbed the menu. "My brain doesn't work on an empty stomach," she said. "Let's order."

— Chapter 90 —

BURGER-TALK at Mel's Drive-in resulted in a gourmet feast for four at The French Laundry, one of the Bay Area's most famous – and costly – restaurants.

Knowing that Cas was not only a fellow publisher, but also an investigative journalist who might help Hallie find information, Tulip had invited Hallie and Cas to dine with her and Pierre at a neighborhood bistro.

Plans changed, however, when Tulip reported that Pierre insisted on hosting the dinner at his favorite restaurant, which turned out to be the French Laundry, a distance away. They set a date for the following Thursday.

Intrigued by Hallie's report of a possible scam artist, Cas was curious as he and Hallie dressed that evening.

"You're sure we're being picked up?" he asked, noticing his wife was sorting through his ties. "Yountville's in the Napa Valley. It's an hour and a half drive when there's no traffic."

"I know, darling. Tulip said that when she told Pierre we were good friends, he wanted to take charge of the evening. What I don't understand is how he got a dinner reservation at the French Laundry. It usually takes at least two months." She handed Cas her choice. "Please wear this with your navy blazer."

He saluted and clicked his heels. "Yes, boss. Anything else?"

"Don't get a spot on it, and don't push food on your fork with your fingers."

"Are you sure we're guests? I hear the place is a money-eating monster. How can a con artist like M'sieu Moulet afford those prices? We'll probably have to do dishes."

"You wash, I'll dry."

"Deal," he said, taking the necktie.

Promptly at the appointed hour of five, a gleaming white limousine pulled up to the Marsh/Casserly residence. The owners watched from a living room window as the driver stopped, open the limo's back door, then helped his passenger out.

"That must be Pierre," Hallie whispered.

"Or whatever name he was born with," murmured Cas.

"Shush, he's coming up the steps."

— Chapter 91 —

MINUTES LATER, driving along the highway, the four passengers had no lack of subjects to chat about. First came the introductions. Hallie said she had a husband and son, loved to read mysteries, and formerly ran a Public Relations firm.

"She's much too modest," said Tulip. "Her family is well-known and highly respected in San Francisco. Her mother, Edith Marsh, has one of the finest collections of

Impressionist art in the country." No mention was made of Hallie's crime-solving skills.

Before Cas could speak, Tulip went on, "Her husband, Dan Casserly, publishes a weekly news magazine. He's won all sorts of journalism awards."

"Most impressive," said Pierre, with a gracious nod. About five-foot-eight in stature, he was meticulously dressed in a navy blue suit topped by a red bow tie. A matching handkerchief graced his pocket. Wisps of hair combed across his balding crown gave the impression he was not enthused about the aging process, yet he looked surprisingly young for fifty-five. His brow was smooth, his round face showed few wrinkles.

Deep-set hazel eyes, fixed intently on whoever was speaking, led Cas to observe, silently, that Pierre bore no resemblance to the handsome, slick, smooth-talking operator his wife had visualized.

"Now it's your turn, M'sieu Moulet," said Hallie. "What brings you to San Francisco?"

"Please, I am Pierre." A slight blush crossed his face as he handed business cards to his three guests. "My company sent me to be here at the commencement. Then I met *Tulipe*."

"He means he first came here on business," said Tulip, tucking the card in her purse.

"Of course," lied Cas, who had pictured his host attending a graduation ceremony. "Your English is terrific, Pierre. I see from your card that you're in the art business?"

"Yes, the most part is Dutch masters of the 17th century."

Hallie brightened. "That would be Rembrandt, *n'est-ce pas?* And Frans Hals, de Grebber, Vermeer. As I recall, they were well celebrated in their lifetimes."

"No, Ms. 'Allie. Johannes Vermeer was first known in Delft, but then forgot for two centuries. Gustav Friedrich Waagen, a German art history writer, renovated him in the 19th century, and today, Vermeer is the most great painter of the Dutch Golden Age."

"Pierre knows *toutes les choses* about art," said Tulip, reaching for his hand.

"My *Tulipe* is very kind, no? I fear I am deep in the ocean when one speaks of art."

"I think you mean a drop," said Tulip. "You're like a drop in the ocean, *mon cher.* But with your knowledge, I'd say you're more like a swimming pool, you know, a *baignoire.*"

Pierre laughed politely. Later, he would ask her why she called him a bathtub.

— Chapter 92 —

TWO-AND-A-HALF HOURS after leaving San Francisco at the peak of rush hour, the white limo pulled up to a pleasant-looking stone building, half-covered with leafy vines. As the passengers stepped out of the long car, three young men and a pretty brunette, all in black suits, emerged from nowhere with smiles, personal greetings by name, and open hands to take coats, hats, whatever.

The head man spoke to Pierre, whispered a few words in his ear, then led him and his party to a single table in an outdoor courtyard. The evening was unusually warm, and still light enough for guests to enjoy the surrounding garden. Hallie complimented Pierre on the table centerpiece of roses, peonies, and of course, tulips.

After drinks and toasts, the maître d' answered the host's request to give a brief history of the premises: "The French Laundry was built in the 1900s as a saloon," he said. "Later, the site became a French steam laundry, then a family diner. In 1994, famous chef Thomas Keller bought this property and created a renowned three-star restaurant here in the wine country."

Seeing Tulip had no wrap, he added, "May I bring you a pashmina scarf, Madame?" She smiled and declined. He then announced that Mr. Moulet had personally selected a ten-course "tasting menu."

As he spoke, a parade of waiters marched in, each holding a small individual portion of the selected delicacy. The menu, printed especially for Mr. Moulet, listed the first course as, "Sabayon of Pearl Tapioca with Island Creek Oysters and White Sturgeon Caviar."

Talk, wine, and tiny-but-tasty courses flowed effortlessly. An hour passed, and Hallie, feeling mellow and relaxed, took advantage of a moment when everyone was eating.

"I'm just curious, Pierre," she said. "Would you mind if I asked you what the maître d' whispered in your ear when we arrived?"

"Not at all," he answered, setting down his fork. "He said he was sorry about Madame Douvier."

Tulip stiffened. "You knew Andi?"

Hallie's quick glance at Cas said, "So he does like rich women!"

"I did not know her well, *chérie*. I take her here one time only. It was not a happy time."

"What happened?" asked Tulip.

"That is not a subject for discussion." He looked across the table and raised his glass. "M'sieu Casserly, have you tasted this '97 Sancerre?"

— Chapter 93 —

HALLIE WAS NOT one to let a question go unanswered. After waiting ten minutes, she excused herself, presumably to visit the restroom, then slipped out the front door.

The white limo was parked at the entrance. The driver stood smoking, then seeing Hallie, stamped out his cigarette.

"Would you tell me something, just between us?" she asked, approaching him. He looked to be in his thirties, with red hair, freckles, and an obsequious manner. "Were you driving Mr. Moulet the night he came here with Andi Douvier?"

"Yes, Ma'am, I was," he said.

She handed him a rolled-up twenty-dollar bill. "Do you remember that night?"

"Why, thank you, Ma'am." He pocketed it. "Yes, I do."

"Something bad happened that night. Do you remember what it was?"

"I'd say 'unfortunate,' not bad, Ma'am. I wouldn't ordinarily talk about it –"

"I promise you no one will know about this conversation."

The driver shifted his weight uneasily. "Well – Ms. Douvier had a lot to drink. She felt sick and asked me to pull off the road. Mr. Moulet was concerned and helped her out of the car. She – uh – vomited on him."

"Right on him?"

"A little on his pants cuffs, mostly his shoes."

"Shoes?" Hallie paused thoughtfully, her imagination spinning. "Omigod," she said, after a moment. "Why the heck didn't I think of that?"

Reaching for the young man's hand, she shook it briskly. "Thank you, thank you, my friend. You may have helped catch a killer."

— Chapter 94 —

THE MOONLIT EVENING ended at half-past ten, as four contented customers began the drive home. Tulip and Pierre sat close together, nuzzling and occasionally kissing. Hallie and Cas pretended not to notice, raving to each other about the food, service, and ambiance.

When the driver finally reached their front door, they said appropriate goodbyes and thank you's, and hurried inside.

A short time later, as Cas was about to climb into bed, Hallie asked him, "Do you think Pierre will have his way with Tulip tonight?"

He laughed. "Your language is so delicate. Yes, I think they will mutually have their way with each other."

"Do you think he's for real?"

"At worst he's a con artist. At best, he's a crafty opportunist whose family has money and deals in art. If he were all he pretends to be, he'd be courting a beautiful young Parisian, not a skinny American woman a decade older."

"Men!" she snorted, wrinkling her nose. "Tulip's bright and attractive, with a lot going for her. And she's not skinny. Did you notice her boobs?"

"I'm married, I'm not dead. Is she rich?"

"She's not hurting. She drives a Bentley, owns a South-of-Market condo, and a beach house in Hawaii. Pierre seems to really like her."

Cas looked heavenward. "The guy's good, I'll give him that. Tulip's being played by an expert. I wonder how our French Romeo latched on to Babe de Baubery. Isn't that where she picked him up?"

"They mutually picked each other up," she corrected, crawling into bed beside him. "I can't wait to call Tulip tomorrow – that is, at the office."

— Chapter 95 —

HALLIE HAD NO NEED to restrain her curiosity. Her phone buzzed at nine the next morning, displaying the name of her caller. "So how are the lovebirds?" she asked.

"Lovebirds, my ass!" Tulip screamed in her ear. "That bastard! That reptile! I hate the son of a bitch!"

"Shhh. Cool down, Tulip. Did you – um – sleep with him?"

"If you can call it that. He was giving orders like a drill sergeant. 'Don't do that, *cherie*, do it thees way. That's correct, *mon amour*, I will train you.' What am I? A dancing bear? Then he had the cojones to tell me he's getting married when he goes back to Paris, but he wants to keep me as his mistress. Can you believe the nerve?"

"Cas was right," Hallie mumbled, under her breath.

"The snake wants to come here twice a year to sell his art," Tulip raged on. "He said he knows I get invited to the best parties, and he'd be my escort. He even mentioned he'd like to see his picture every month in the *Star*. I was so mad I handed him the champagne he brought, batted my lashes and said, 'Do me a favor, sweetie, and go screw yourself?' He thought I wanted him to open the bottle!"

Hallie burst into laughter and after a few seconds, Tulip joined her.

"*C'est la vie, ma chère Tulipe,* but fortunately, no harm done, except maybe to your ego. At least we all had a nice dinner. Did you ever ask him how he got a table so fast?"

"Yes, the louse said he makes an April reservation every January, then he comes here and decides what lucky female merits the thrill of his company that night. Last year it was poor Andi. God knows what went wrong. She probably got drunk."

"Right on. The driver told me she threw up on Moulet."

"Really? Good for Andi! If she were around, I'd thank her. By the way, what's happening there? Any news?"

"Not at the moment." Hallie paused. "But if I'm

191

right – before too long, we may be getting some answers."

— Chapter 96 —

LATER THAT FRIDAY MORNING, Hallie phoned TB, leaving a message to please call back. Monday afternoon, he responded.

"You asked me to help you with the Douvier case," she reminded him gently, "and I thank you for sharing the names of the wine theft suspects. I wanted to suggest to you that because you checked the soles of their shoes, we shouldn't assume that they aren't murder suspects. One couple filed for divorce right after Andi's party. Makes you wonder what triggered it. Another woman on that list lost her seat on the Opera Board when Andi replaced her."

"That's worth killing for?"

"Some might think so. We know that on the night of her party, Andi was looking for a break in the railing where she could lean over the deck and vomit. She was apparently able to hold it in until she got to the chain in the gangway. We assume that she stopped there and let go. My point is that whoever pushed Andi into the water had to be standing close to her when she upchucked. It's very likely some particles landed on his shoes – that is, the front of his or her shoes."

"Are you suggesting we check the shoes again?"

"That's exactly what I'm suggesting. You were wise to hold onto them. You checked the bottoms, the soles, now you should check the tops, even the laces if there are any, to look for residues of –"

"Vomitus."

"Yes. I realize it's another long shot, but to be honest, some of those people on your wine list could have motives. We have so few leads, let's at least eliminate them as suspects."

"Jesus." TB heaved a sigh. "Those lab guys are going to kill me. Can't we just do the ones who sound suspicious? Who are they?"

"My instincts aren't reliable. It could also be someone who doesn't sound suspicious. You collected the shoes right after the murder, so even if the culprit cleaned them, there could still be infinitesimal particles not visible to the naked eye, couldn't there?"

"I'll get back to you," he said wearily, and clicked off.

PART 14

THE LATE AFTERNOON sun beamed down on Crissy Field, a National Park alongside the bay, and favorite walking path for locals. Sara Redington ran down the trail, wheeling a contented Danny in his stroller, while Hallie kept pace beside her. Then suddenly Hallie stopped.

"Whoa!" she said, gasping for breath. "Let's cool it awhile. I can't keep up with you young chicks."

"Okay, Grandma." Sara paused to straighten her sun hat, then continued walking slowly along the path. "By the way, Hal, I keep forgetting to tell you I saw the grieving husband a few nights ago."

"You mean Andi's grieving husband?"

"In person. I recognized him from his pictures. He's quite a hunk."

"He's could also be a wife-killer. Where was he?"

"Walgreen's – in Laurel Village."

"Buying condoms?"

Sara laughed. "I wasn't that close."

"He probably gets them by the bushel. Was he alone?"

"Yes, in the store. But I saw him drive by as I was walking to my car. Someone was with him."

"Female, no doubt."

"I couldn't tell. You seem awfully interested for a happily married woman."

"I am," Hallie said, taking back Danny's stroller and pushing it. "I'm happily married and I'm also interested. I'm going crazy trying to think of what I missed in this damn case. I've been over every possible aspect of the murder, and some things don't add up. I have several suspects in mind, but I can't seem to put it all together. What's wrong with me?"

"You're trying too hard. You're practically obsessing. Why don't you cool it for a while and let the police worry about it?"

"Good idea. Speaking of cool, might you be interested in our favorite ice cream place?"

"Mmm – butter toffee with caramel dip. What are we waiting for?" Sara stepped around a group of pigeons feasting on breadcrumbs. "Just as I thought. Exercise is for the birds."

— Chapter 98 —

THE NEXT DAY, on her way downtown to St. Anthony's, Hallie passed the Douvier mansion on Washington Street. Would Nick Demetropolis still be living there, she wondered – then doubted it. The upkeep on the estate, the property taxes, the help's salaries alone would deplete almost any bank account.

As she drove by, a man emerged from the front door, walking quickly, carrying two large suitcases.

Pulling up to the curb, pretending to park, Hallie recognized the "grieving husband" in her rear view mirror. He seemed in a hurry as he dumped the suitcases in the trunk of his blue Maserati, climbed inside, and whizzed past her.

Where would Nick be going with all that baggage at 11:20 in the morning? She remembered Helen Kaiser saying that Megin Dixon lived in Pacific Heights. Were they still seeing each other? Without stopping to think, she decided to follow him as he drove down to Geary Street, then headed west towards the Pacific Ocean.

Anxious to keep him in sight, she trailed close behind for another mile, until he surprised her by taking a sharp right. Traffic was light, and she knew she risked being spotted, but she turned and stayed with him three more blocks. Then, suddenly, he stopped in the middle of a quiet street, blocking her way.

Jumping out, he strode up to her car window, glaring. "Why the hell are you – oh, for God's sake, it's you, Cinderella!" His frown dissolved into a smile. "Why didn't you say you wanted to get together? I guess the chase is always exciting. But now that you've caught me, where shall we go for lunch?"

Hallie rolled down her window. "I owe you an apology, Mr. D," she said, blushing. "I've been studying your wife's case for a long time, and when I saw you come out of your house, I just – I guess impulsively – decided to see where you were going."

"Did you find out?"

"Not really. Maybe to see Megin?"

"I don't like talking this way, Hallie," he said. "That's your name, isn't it? I'm Nick. If you'd consider parking in that space over there, and coming with me to the Cliff House, I'll not only answer your question, I'll catch you up on recent developments in this case."

The offer of new information was irresistible. She also knew that one didn't get into cars with murder suspects.

"Suppose I meet you at the Cliff House?"

"Splendid." To her relief, he climbed into his front seat. "See you there!" he called.

— Chapter 99 —

THE VALET PARKER at the entrance to the Cliff House helped Hallie out of her car and handed her a ticket.

"Do I pay now?" she asked as he slipped a tag under her windshield wiper.

"Mr. D already took care of you, Miss. He treats his ladies real good."

"I am *not* one of his 'ladies!' " She gritted her teeth. "I am simply an acquaintance who's trying to find out what happened to his wife."

"My mistake, Miss. I did think you were kinda old for him. That is –"

"No problem," she said, laughing to herself.

The Cliff House, a huge white building perched on a bluff at the end of Ocean Beach, was a longtime mecca for tourists, as well as a favorite of locals. The view overlooked three-and-a-half miles of sandy shore, a seemingly endless expanse of ocean, and the famous Seal Rocks, where the mammals swam and frolicked.

Nick Demetropoulos, waiting inside the crowded entrance, spotted his guest instantly, took her arm and led her down a flight of stairs to Sutro's, a stunning, modern-designed restaurant. A pretty hostess greeted him with a wink, and seated them at a corner table.

"Spectacular," said Hallie, peering through the sky-high windows.

"Yes, you are." He beamed at her.

"Save it, Nick. The valet parker told me I was too old for you."

"Well, you might be," he teased. "Are you thirty yet?"

"Who cares? I'm a happy wife and mother. You're handsome, charming, single, rich – and I'm here strictly on business."

"Of course you are," he smiled. "And you can relax. I don't go near married women anymore. You see before you a new me."

"Oh?"

"Andi's death changed everything for me, and not always for the better. Despite our differences, she was my great love, as well as my protection against certain females who wanted that terrible C-word."

"Commitment."

"Precisely. And so, no, I don't see Megin anymore. She's gone all hoity-toity anyway."

"I read that Andi left each of you $5 million."

He gave a shrug. "I guess it's no secret now. She also left her clothes and scarves and jewelry – all that crap – to Megin. And she left me the house and grounds. I just turned down an offer of $65 million from some Silicon Valley kid, not even old enough to be my grandson."

Hallie was stunned. "Did you know Andi was leaving you the house?"

"Yes, we talked about it." He handed her the menu. "Does that give me a motive for murder?"

"I don't know, Nick. Did you kill her?"

"No," he said emphatically. "Shall we order?"

— Chapter 100 —

CONVERSATION FLOWED EASILY and the more Nick talked, the more questions Hallie had. Why had he wanted the news of his inheritance kept secret? What caused the breakup with Megin? Was he serious about Andi being his "great love"? And most important, what about his alibi?

Her memories of that short meeting on the ship were vague. She had told the police that he was with her at the time of the murder, but was she sure of the timing? He hadn't yet found his table that evening. Where had he been just before they met?

Suspicions were mounting. And now he had a multi-million dollar motive.

A call to TB as soon as she got home that afternoon brought a speedy reply. "What is it, Hallie?" the detective asked impatiently.

"I just had lunch with Mr. Demetropoulos," she said. "He was coming out of the house he now owns on Washington Street."

"Andi's house? He bought it?"

"He inherited it – from Andi. He knew she was leaving it to him. I think it gives him a motive. Also, I vouched for his presence – with me – at the time of the murder. Now I'm not so sure of the timing."

"What changed your mind?"

"Thinking about it."

"Good work. We'll take any leads we can get. Email me what you think we should ask Mr. D, and we'll bring him in for questioning. By the way, you suggested testing the front of the wine suspects' shoes for vomit. I told Lieutenant Kaiser about it because I thought it was so – frankly, stupid – and she told me to do it anyway."

"We scored a hit?"

"Hold on, Hallie. Two pairs were positive for traces of vomitus – but the shoes had all been washed and cleaned since Andi's party, and the quantity of emesis we got from each shoe is the size of a pinpoint. The lab guys knocked themselves out to get enough for a DNA sample."

"Whose shoes were they?"

"I'll let you know when and if one of the samples matches Andi's DNA."

"When will you know? I have a possible suspect in mind."

"Forget it. One of the crew members confessed to stealing the wine, so we solved that mystery."

"Good for you, TB. But I wasn't talking about the wine. I'm thinking that one of the people on your list might be our killer."

"Well, keep thinking," he said. "We need all the suspects we can get. And don't forget to send me whatever you learned about Mr. D. By the way, why were you having lunch with the guy?"

"All in a day's work."

"Okay," he said. "I'll call you."

Chapter 101

HALLIE LOST no time sending a list of questions to TB. A week later, she received his report:

"*Tuesday, April 30ʰ 2013: SFPD Case 0812-5534D, the murder of Alexandra 'Andi' Douvier; interview with victim's husband, Nicholas J. Demetropoulos, aka Mr. D, age 49.*

"*Suspect was friendly and cooperative, answering questions partly suggested by private citizen/amateur crime-solver Hallie Marsh. Asked why he had withheld information about inheriting his late wife's multi-million dollar home and grounds, he replied that it was his personal business and he was under no obligation to publicize the results of her will.*

"*Despite the large bequest, he insisted and gave reasons why his life was 'far better' when the victim was alive. He appeared to be truthful, and not in great need of money. Bank records showed a positive balance and no recent past or current debts.*

"*In response to the question about his friendship with Ms. Megin Dixon, he replied that, 'We just grew apart.' Suspect became noticeably uncomfortable, however, when asked about his alibi for the time of his wife's murder. He explained that he had been using the bathroom in his cabin before going up to the dining room, where he met and spoke with Ms. Marsh. (She had originally said they were chatting at the time of the murder, but she recently recanted, saying she couldn't be sure about the timing.)*

"*Suspect was asked if anyone had seen him going to or from his cabin, or could verify his story. Thanks to Detective*

Brisco's determined interrogation, the suspect (reluctantly) told Detectives Baer and Brisco that a lady was with him in his cabin at the time, 'a lovely Greek waitress from the ship. I think her name was Athena.'

"A radiogram to the ship Medusa reported back that Athena Gounarias at first denied being with Mr. D, but on learning that he could be tried for murder if she could not corroborate his story, admitted being in his cabin. Since she was not supposed to be there, she remembered checking her watch, and confirmed that they were 'together' at the time of the homicide.

"At this moment, there is no further need to question Mr. D."

Hallie smiled as she read the report. The pieces were finally beginning to fit. TB deserved a call of thanks.

He answered his phone and spoke first. "I was about to call you, Hallie," he said. "Good news! The vomitus on one of the shoes matched Andi's DNA."

"Was it a black Ferragamo loafer?"

"How the hell did you know that?"

"Congratulations, TB. I believe you've caught our killer."

— Chapter 102 —

ONCE AGAIN, Hallie stood with Lieutenant Kaiser outside the small, soundproof Interrogation Room in the police station.

Inside, the walls were free of decoration save for the

one-way mirror which permitted others to watch and hear the questioning. Four chairs and a square desk were the only furniture.

TB, the interrogator, took a seat opposite the suspect, while Lenny sat across from a stern-looking lawyer named Colbert.

The elderly attorney was instantly on the offensive. "So, officers, what's all this nonsense about my client committing a murder?"

"It's not nonsense, Colbert." TB spoke in a quiet voice. "We have forensic evidence tying Mr. Robinson directly to the body."

"Dried snot on his shoe? You call that evidence?"

"Dried vomitus," corrected Lenny, turning to the suspect. "Your shoe, Mr. Robinson, had Andi's DNA on it."

"Andi Douvier was a junkie, a drunk, and a bulimic." Wallace Robinson leaned forward on his chair. "She threw up once before when I was serving drinks at a party. Spilled her guts all over Mrs. Thornwell's Karastan carpet. Got it on my tux, too."

"I'll do the talking, Wallace," said Colbert firmly. He had faced the homicide detectives before. Their routine was familiar; he was not about to let Lenny badger his client.

"We have witnesses," the lawyer went on, "who will attest to the fact that Ms. Douvier 'purged herself' on a previous occasion where my client was performing his butler duties. You can't possibly pinpoint the date when that speck of material landed on his shoe."

"Oh, but we can," said Lenny. "The vomitus was a tiny fragment of whey cheese known as Myzithra. This particular brand was a secret blend of goat's and sheep's milk made only in Thessaly, Greece. It's not available in this country."

Colbert laughed. "Is that the best you can do? Very creative, I'll give you that – especially since there was no food in Ms. Douvier's stomach."

"None to speak of," said TB. "But the chef on the ship remembers Ms. Douvier came into the galley before the guests arrived, to check on the hors d'oeuvres. He offered her a cracker with Myzithra on it and she took a small bite."

Lenny thrust a paper at the lawyer. "Here's how to reach Chef Gaston aboard the Medusa. He'll be happy to confirm what we just told you."

"Ridiculous," said Colbert. "Penal Law Section –"

A knock on the door interrupted him. "Excuse us," said TB. "We'll be right back."

— Chapter 103 —

"WHAT'S GOING ON, LIEUTENANT?" asked TB, once they'd closed the door behind them. His tone said that he did not like to be disturbed during questioning.

"Colbert's a tough old fart," she answered. "Hallie has a suggestion."

"Hallie?" He turned to her. "What?"

"Remember the poisoned doves? Right after the tragedy, when I was talking to Wallace about the poor birds, he made a strange remark, and I wrote it down. He said, 'I've wondered what kind of person could be that cruel.' "

"Person?"

"Exactly. At the time I thought it was strange. No one knew the birds had been poisoned. You told me not to tell anyone, and I never did. As far as everyone knew, they died of heat exhaustion."

"A good observation," said Lenny, "but hardly evidence."

"I'm not so sure." Hallie was getting excited. "I think Wallace put poison in the birdseed knowing they'd get sick or die. He wanted to create a distraction."

"Why?" asked TB.

Hallie brushed back a wave of hair. "I'm guessing he somehow got a key to Andi's cabin. He knew she was paranoid about her jewelry and usually carried it in her purse, which would be locked in the room."

"Speculation," said Lenny.

TB put his finger to his lips. "Go on, Hallie."

"Lenny's right, it is speculation," she agreed. "But I think Andi may have surprised him in her cabin. Everyone was talking about the birds, and he didn't think she'd leave her guests during the crisis, especially since she was sitting at the Captain's Table."

"Go on."

"Some way or other," Hallie continued, "Andi saw Wallace had taken her pearls. Maybe he had them in his hands, or bulging out of a pocket. She grabbed them, put them on, then threatened to report him."

"We're listening," said TB.

"Okay, so he followed her to the deck – maybe pleaded with her – all the way to the gangway railing. When she got there, she began retching, and some vomit got on his shoe, which he later cleaned."

"You forgot the punch line," said Lenny. "He struck her on the head with a wooden weapon, and pushed her into the bay."

"It's still theory," said the Lieutenant. "It might explain the pearls, but we can't prove anything without an eyewitness."

"Wallace doesn't know that," said TB.

Lenny shook his head. "Colbert won't fall for a bluff."

"But Wallace might." TB patted Hallie's shoulder. "Thanks, Miss Snoopy. I think you may be on to something."

— Chapter 104 —

BACK IN THE INTERROGATION ROOM, TB apologized for the interruption. Colbert looked concerned; Wallace seemed relieved.

"Everyone's got something to say," sighed TB, "and it always has to be right away. It can't wait ten minutes."

Wallace chuckled. "America's the only country in the world where people look at a microwave and say, 'Faster! Faster!'"

"That's true," said TB, forcing a smile. "So, Mr. Robinson. We were just informed we have a witness who claims he saw you on deck the night of Andi's party."

"And we have witnesses," Colbert snapped, "who'll confirm that my client was washing dishes and never left the galley that night."

Wallace squirmed uncomfortably. "I might've come

up for air for a few seconds," he said. "That galley got awfully stuffy."

Colbert shot him a mean look. "I'm doing the talking, remember?"

TB grabbed his advantage. "When do you think you might have popped outside for a few seconds?"

"Sometime before dinner," said Wallace.

"He means after dinner," Colbert corrected. "His memory's failing."

"The hell it is," Wallace said. "There's not a damn thing wrong with my memory!"

"Shut up, Wallace."

"I won't shut up, Colbert. I've a right to defend myself."

"Our witness seemed to think you saw Andi that night," said TB, before Colbert could stop him.

"Honestly, I was just trying to help her, detective. She wasn't feeling well – she was full of cocaine and vodka and God knows what else. She could hardly walk. I just wanted to help her."

"Is that why you stole her pearls?" asked Lenny.

"Now hold on!" shouted Colbert. "I need time alone with my client. *Please!*"

"Of course," said TB, standing up. "Just give a yell when you're ready."

— Chapter 105 —

THIS TIME, re-entering the Interrogation Room, the detectives found a pale, frightened suspect. His fingers were trembling as he asked, "You officers are allowed to lie to me, right?"

TB's hand shot up to silence Lenny.

"Colbert told you correctly, Wallace," TB answered. "On occasion, police are allowed to employ deceptive tactics in the belief that an innocent person wouldn't confess to something he or she didn't do."

"Damn right!" Lenny went into his act. "But it's no lie that you poisoned those birds so you could sneak into Andi's cabin and steal her pearls. We –"

"I wasn't going to steal her pearls," Wallace said angrily. "I was just looking around her cabin to make sure everything was in order."

Colbert threw up his hands. "Keep talking, Wallace. I'll come visit you in San Quentin."

"I'm not going to prison! Andi was wearing her pearls when she died, so how could I have stolen them? I didn't steal anything. It was all an accident – a terrible accident. I tried to save her!"

"An accident? That changes everything," added Lenny, quietly sarcastic.

TB glared at his partner. "You're doing fine, Wallace," he said. "You'll feel better if you get it off your chest."

Colbert was angry. "You detectives are putting extreme pressures on my client. He's not going to say another word."

"Sure he is," said TB. "You can't take away his freedom of speech."

"I *want* to talk and clear myself," Wallace protested. "You can't throw me in jail for trying to do something nice for the birds. I love animals, all sorts. Ask anybody. Yeah, I put chocolate in the birdseed; I thought it would be a treat for the little doves."

How did he know it was the chocolate that poisoned them, TB wondered, but thought it best not to interrupt.

"I'm telling the truth," Wallace went on. "Earlier that evening, the Chief Engineer knew I was part of the catering staff, and gave me an orchid plant and a key to Andi's cabin. He asked me put it on her coffee table while she was at dinner."

"You were following orders," said TB.

"That's what I'm paid big bucks to do." He smiled. "Say, may I use your restroom?"

"Certainly," said Lenny, getting up. "Follow me."

— Chapter 106 —

TEN MINUTES LATER, back in the Interrogation Room, Wallace tried to sound jovial. "Geez, you cops won't even let a guy pee in peace." He looked at Lenny. "Did you think I was going to run off?"

Lenny frowned. "Rules are rules."

"Please sit down, Wallace," said Colbert. "Detective Baer and I have been talking. I think you should tell him exactly what happened that night, and we may be able to work out a deal."

"What kind of deal?"

"They'll take the death penalty off the table."

"WHOA! What death penalty? For an accident?"

Colbert sighed. "Tell them what happened, Wallace."

"Damn right!" He pressed his lips together. "It was just like I said. I went to Andi's cabin to deliver the orchid plant, not to steal anything. She's so damn paranoid; everyone knows that. Her pearls were sitting on a table and she didn't think she'd left them there. She put them around her neck and said she was going to tell the caterer I was trying to steal them."

The room was silent.

"She ran up to the deck," he went on. "Sure, I followed her. If the city's biggest caterer blacklisted me, I'd never work again. I begged her not to say anything but she just kept staggering 'round the deck holding onto the railing. When she got to the gangway chain, she squatted down and got down on her hands and knees and threw up into the water. I guess that's when some stuff splashed onto my shoes."

"Why did you hit her?" asked TB.

"I didn't mean to hurt her. I was just trying to get her attention. I wanted her to say she wasn't going to turn me in. I had this wooden tray that I used to carry the orchid plant. I tapped her lightly on the back of her head. She kept throwing up – I couldn't stop her. The next thing I know, she slipped under the chain and fell into the bay."

"Why didn't you call for help?" asked Lenny.

"Everyone was at dinner – eating it or serving it. I knew she wouldn't survive the icy water long enough for me to run and try to find someone. I didn't mean to hurt her. That's the truth. I swear it!"

"Thanks, Wallace." TB looked at Colbert. "Blunt force trauma. No justification. Murder one."

"No premeditation. Mitigating factors," countered the lawyer. "Man two, we leave sentencing to the judge."

"Cuff him, Lenny," sighed a weary TB. "And read him his rights."

— Chapter 107 —

"THE BUTLER DID IT?" Cas looked up from his computer. Hallie had just come back from the police station.

"Yup. Confession and all."

"You can tell me about it later. What's for dinner?"

"Oops! I'm sorry, I forgot to go shopping. What's in the fridge?"

"Three oranges, stale bread and Jenny's doggie bag from her date last night. She says she has a headache and isn't hungry."

"Hmm." Hallie took a moment to think. "I wouldn't feel quite right feasting on our nanny's doggie bag. You should've married Helen Kaiser. She told me she loves to cook."

"I didn't marry you for your cooking skills – or lack of same. We could go out for dinner."

"I'm too tired. Did you happen to peek in Jenny's doggie bag?"

"I did. Spaghetti and meatballs, untouched by human hands. Enough for two."

"Do you think she'd mind?"

"She eats our food. Why shouldn't we eat hers?"

"Good thinking, darling. Race you to the kitchen."